Love is
a time of enchantment:
in it all days are fair and all fields
green. Youth is blest by it,
old age made benign:
the eyes of love see
roses blooming in December,
and sunshine through rain. Verily
is the time of true-love
a time of enchantment — and
Oh! how eager is woman
to be bewitched!

YASMIN

Elaine understood that she was to be the governess at Reynauld Hall in Cornwall, but on her journey westward she quickly discovered that Sir Edward Reynauld was not to be trusted. She came into a house in which voices whispered one name . . . Yasmin. The past echoed and teased. Why did Sir Edward fear the gipsy's curse? Why did Elaine's friendship with Robert Polkerris have to be kept secret? Who was Yasmin, and why did she fill Elaine's life?

ANNE LOWING

YASMIN

Complete and Unabridged

ULVERSCROFT
Leicester

First published in Great Britain in 1969

First Large Print Edition
published November 1995

British Library CIP Data

Lowing, Anne
  Yasmin.—Large print ed.—
  Ulverscroft large print series: romance
  I. Title
  823.914 [F]

ISBN 0-7089-3419-6

Published by
F. A. Thorpe (Publishing) Ltd.
Anstey, Leicestershire
Set by Words & Graphics Ltd.
Anstey, Leicestershire
Printed and bound in Great Britain by
T. J. Press (Padstow) Ltd., Padstow, Cornwall

This book is printed on acid-free paper

1

AS I stand alone in this unfrequented spot near the churchyard wall, I wonder whether people will ever allow themselves to forget the man who lies buried here. The silence around me is unnatural. My eyes seek the feathered presence of wild birds but they seem to shun the hedges and lone elm, while the air is still without their song. Yes, in the distance, I can hear them calling to one another with joy on this beautiful spring day. Farther away, the tranquil sea murmurs gently after the rages of winter.

I have been told that the villagers rarely take the narrow lane which borders this part of the churchyard; instead, they prefer to travel a longer route rather than pass so close to this dreaded place. Can it be that they still fear him? But what is there to fear from a man who has been dead these years?

Today the village is different; happier

than I have ever known it. Smiles brighten the faces of the men and their good wives; while everyone appears content and well fed. The cottages are in good repair, and the torn sacking hammered over the glassless windows has been discarded for good. Behind the closed doors comes the sound of gaiety and laughter, reminding me poignantly of those heart-rending cries to which I had become accustomed whenever I came to the village.

I cannot even trace the borders of the grave with my foot: weeds and wild flowers have grown in such profusion that I suspect Nature of trying to hide all traces of the wounds. Once the memory of the man who lies beneath this greenery was stark, but Time has now softened remembrances. The plain headstone leans drunkenly to one side, and the sharp outline of its lettering has been dulled by the bobbling moss which grows upon it. No mischievous boy has dared to carve his name or initials on the hard granite, for fear the ghost of the departed shall rise and haunt him.

Before I came to the churchyard I visited the house. I cannot explain what force drew me to the massive gateway, because originally I had had no intention of setting my foot on such ground. Had he been with me, I know my husband would have done his utmost to dissuade me from going to the house. When first I had told him of my wish to return to the village, he had frowned, questioning the wisdom of such an urge. It had been with reluctance that finally he had agreed to allow me to come to the village. Had I not suffered enough during the time I had lived here?

The fine iron gates had been taken away and now one large supporting pillar was badly cracked; almost as if a cart had been backed into it, or a vicious frost had extended its penetrating fingers into tiny fissures, to wrench and twist until the stone had given way under the immense force. On passing through the gateway I had paused to look about me. Everything seemed so terribly desolate! The fine gravel of the carriageway could no longer be seen under the unruly carpet of grass and weeds which abounded, and the erstwhile tidy flower beds did not exist. Wildness ran riot. Even the trees above my head and the bushes at my side seemed forlorn, their budspikes not yet swollen in the process of re-birth. Was it possible that Nature had forgotten this place, or was she reluctant to touch it with her healing hands?

I wandered slowly up the carriageway, while my heart pounded within my breast. Was it possible for me still to experience an ancient terror?

I shuddered involuntarily when I caught sight of the ruins of the house. My hands sought each other in a firm clasp, and my lips parted. Then a tremendous wave of compassion swept over me and tears blurred my vision. Bricks and mortar cannot be responsible for the evil hearts that dwell within them! This had once been such a proud and beautiful house. Now the stonework crumbled, the carvings had been rendered almost featureless, and some lintels had fallen from above the gaping window sockets. Over all, ivy and creeper triumphed; clinging, strangling, rapacious in their conquest of man's folly, yet soothing with their balm of forgetfulness. In a few years time, the stains of black would be completely hidden by greenery, until the final stones crumbled into dust to leave nothing . . . nothing.

I found myself beside the remains of a stone bench, which previously had served as a resting-place for those who wished to admire the fish gliding in the pond. Of that water-filled basin, there was little more to be seen than a small dip in the level of the ground. I sat down and stared at the house. I knew that if I stepped beyond the gaping portal I should be standing on the charred timberwork of the upper floors and roof rafters. I was unable to resist my curiosity and rose again to my feet. With hastening pulse, I stepped over the threshold and paused to look about me.

Above my head the sun came out from behind a thin wisp of cloud and threw the shadows in sharp relief. I traced the line of the wall, the bright square of light that had been a window, and then the darkness again where the stonework continued. My eyes saw a ruin, while my mind the house in its former splendour. Then I smiled as I looked at my own shadow. I raised my head and called out:

"Is all well, Yasmin?"

Had I expected a reply? No, I do not think so.

The breeze stirred amongst the winter-dried twigs of a nearby oak and a blackbird in a tree some distance away rent the air with his gay call. There was an air of peace and tranquillity about the house and I was content. After so many long, dreadful years, the shades had been lifted.

I stand here by the grave, thinking back to that dull, cold and drenching day in late November when both blade and branch had been overweighed with saturation. They had placed me at this side, with my back to the sea, and the wind had eaten into my back, chilling me to the bone.

But that was just the end . . .

★ ★ ★

I came to a halt in the middle of the cobbled street and bent down to lift the stumbling small girl who had caused the entire crocodile to fall into confusion behind her.

6

"Priscilla!" I scolded. "How many times have I to tell you to keep looking front whilst walking? Now look what you've done to Bessie and the others! Come quickly, child, before we are run down by a carriage."

The other ten girls giggled mischievously and I could see that plump red-haired Bessie was nudging her nearest companion. Then I heard her whisper:

"He's here again!"

Involuntarily, my eyes flickered towards the buildings on the other side of the street, and my heart seemed to miss a beat. As Bessie had rightly proclaimed, the man was standing there, watching us. I knew I had begun to blush and hastily averted my gaze, fussing about the girls like a mother-hen.

"Into line again, please. Quickly, Jane. Susan!"

"Yes, Miss."

"Of course, Miss."

With a great deal of unnecessary pushing and jostling, my charges once again took up their position. My hand was still on Priscilla's arm, and I moved her to the rear of the crocodile.

"You had better walk here, Priscilla," I told her, "then if you stumble again, you won't hold up the remainder of us."

I took my place at their head and our tiny procession went on its way again. We were within thirty yards of the high stone walls which surrounded the establishment that housed, fed and cared for us. As we drew closer, our steps seemed to falter; it was as if we were reluctant to reincarcerate ourselves. I had been conscious of this dread for over a year and I believed my charges sensed my feelings, although no word was ever spoken.

"Come, girls!" I said brightly. "We must not be late for supper." This meal consisted of meagre bowls of thin broth, helped down by bread crusts, and was eaten at five o'clock exactly.

I leaned against the heavy iron gate and pushed it wide, before standing aside to allow the crocodile to pass through. I raised my eyes slightly, until I was able to read the rusting metal words set in the arc above my head:

When the last pupil had entered the courtyard, I carefully closed the gate and fastened the padlock. I took a key from beneath the folds of my skirt and turned it in the lock. This world of ours was like a prison; the only thing missing is the barred window, I thought. Life beyond these high, confining walls is not for us. Then I wondered if I should ever leave the place, or whether I was doomed to remain here until I became too old to teach.

Before I turned to trace my steps back into the house, my eyes alighted on the stranger who was now standing on the far side of the street. My heart skipped a beat. Why had he followed us here? I asked myself in panic. What does he want with us?

I had heard all the stories about undesirable characters who roamed the streets, who haunted the back alleys, who begged, borrowed or stole; the cut-throats, procurers, and other unsavoury people; and, for the first time in my life,

I was thankful for the heavy, padlocked gate that separated us.

I could not drag my eyes away from his face! Thick eyebrows, hard lines about the mouth and that large, dis-figuring birthmark stretching from the corner of his left eye to the middle of his cheek . . . rather like a ragged crescent moon. It was a vivid red in colour, otherwise I doubt whether I should have been able to see it from such a distance.

I felt my face burn with fire, and then saw the corners of his mouth lift in a derisory smile. The spell broken, I clutched my skirts in my hands and almost ran towards the front door where the girls were awaiting me. They were giggling and nudging each other. I scowled. A voice from my left murmured:

"Is he your follower, Miss?"

"I don't know what you're talking about!" I snapped back, my face burning with mortification. "'You will oblige me by going straight to your dormitory and removing your shawls and pattens. Diana! Kindly stop smirking and compose your lips!"

10

They hastened to obey my order, pushing and jostling in their youthful haste to enter the house. Then the feet of eleven girls, ranging in age from seven to twelve, clattered across the stone floor towards the staircase. Mindful of the ever-open door to Mrs. Crane's private room, I called after them:

"No talking!" before hurrying up the stairs to my own tiny room under the eaves. I tossed my plain bonnet on to the narrow, hard truckle-bed and then crossed to the window. By craning my neck, I could just see into the street beneath. I twisted from left to right, but there was no sign of the stranger. Half-eager, half-afraid, I wondered if he would be out there waiting for us on the morrow. I turned from the window and walked slowly back to the bed to sit down and remove my outdoor footwear. A draught howled across the floor under an ill-fitting door.

It was a horrible poky bedroom, but I knew I ought to have been thankful for its bare, damp walls, low ceiling and jutting corners. Mrs. Crane might have insisted on my sharing another room with one of the maids, whose quarters were even worse than my own. I must be grateful for small mercies, I reminded myself. At least I had been spared the humiliation of squeezing into the airless cupboard beneath the back stairs which housed Ninette, the scullion whose physique and stature were so deformed and shrunken that she was able to fit quite comfortably into a clock-case.

The following day was overcast and the light filtering through the tiny windows of the classroom so poor, that I was tempted to light the tallow candles in order to save my dear pupils' eyes from severe strain. However, prudence stayed my hand, and I was obliged to content myself with helping the girls move the benches closer to the window. We had barely seated ourselves and taken up our work, when the door was thrown open and Mrs. Crane stood there, resplendent in her bombazine glory. Eleven pairs of eyes were swiftly averted, while the same number of hands laid down their needlework, and a chorus of young voices said in a polite tone:

"Good day, Madam."

"I want you!" A long, bony finger pointed in my direction. "Downstairs immediately. You may leave Clarissa in charge until your return."

"I, Madam?" I echoed, searching my mind for a possible misdemeanour.

"Are you deaf, girl? Come!" She held the door wide before turning back to inspect the class. "How dare you move the benches without my permission! Clarissa Trundell!" The girl thus addressed jumped to her feet, spilling her needlework on to the floor. "See that everyone returns to their correct positions. And don't stand there gawking, girl! Your threads are getting dirty and muddled." She glared at me. "Have you succeeded in teaching them anything at all, I wonder?"

I held my tongue . . . as was expected of me . . . then followed Mrs. Crane along the dark passage leading to the staircase and ground floor. Her skirts rustled along the bare boards, and it seemed to me that their very tone registered her displeasure. I reviewed my recent actions in an effort to find any cause for disharmony.

13

Outside the door of her sitting-room, Mrs. Crane paused to give me a withering, contemptuous glance. Then her nostrils curled as she accused in a low voice:

"Doubtless you already know about this!"

She flung wide the door and my eyes alighted on the figure within the room. He was standing beside the hideous marble fireplace, one velvet sleeve supported by the mantelpiece. His face turned towards me and I gasped involuntarily.

It was the man I had seen in the street!

Her eyes as beady as black buttons, Mrs. Crane whispered in triumph:

"Then you do know all about this! Scheming, ungrateful hussy!" Suddenly her face changed, becoming wreathed in friendly smiles. Her fat arm slid around my shoulders and she urged me forward, until we were both standing in front of the stranger.

"Here she is, Sir Edward!" she cooed, her voice as smooth and oily as if she had swallowed a quart of castor oil. "This is my dear, dear Elaine." She spun me round to face her, and I hated the insincere smirk in her eyes as she continued:

"I don't know how I shall manage without her! She's been an absolute treasure to me, Sir Edward! Yes, an absolute *treasure!*" Then her finger-nails closed over the thin fabric of my drab grey dress, and I could not help wincing with pain. "Come, my dear, allow me to introduce you to your new employer. Elaine, this is Sir Edward Reynauld, of Reynauld Hall, in Cornwall." She released me and flung up her arms in a mock flutter, trilling with a sham laugh:

"He! He! Such excitement! Such a tremendous honour! To leave my most humble and modest little orphanage to work for this illustrious gentleman! Naturally I have told him of your antecedents, my dear, for it would not do to allow a complete *Nobody* to accept the post of governess to his beloved daughter. There!" She turned to me in triumph. "I cannot believe I have surprised you at all, Elaine! Naughty girl!" she cooed in my face, her eyes flashing with an anger which could not be seen by the third person in the room. "Why ever did you seek to hide such facts from me? After all, am I not your dear, good, kind confidante and mentor, who took you out of a cruel, cruel world when your sweet mother died? And have I not kept you on here to teach my other dear little girls because your money ran out? Surely you could have repaid me by informing me of this sudden alliance?" She laughed again and her fat hand touched my cheek. I felt the hatred in her person. "However, we must all have our little girlish secrets, mustn't we, Sir Edward? I am not in the least cross with this dear girl!"

I longed only for the floor to open and swallow me up. I knew that, later, I should be receiving the full lash of Mrs. Crane's tongue. No matter how much I protested, I knew she would not believe I had had nothing at all to do with this unexpected offer.

She smiled again and left my side to lay her beringed fingers upon Sir Edward Reynauld's right arm. She lowered her eyelashes in an attempt to be coy and amusing; one that I found nauseating in the highest degree.

"Dear Sir Edward!" she gushed at him; while he, I noticed, appeared completely bored, disinterested, and revulsed. "Sir Edward has compensated me so generously for the abrupt loss of your services, Elaine. Ah yes! Had it not been for the difficulty I shall experience whilst trying to find a replacement worthy of your own loyalty and skill, I should not have permitted him to take you from me. Naturally I shall not stand in your way, child! Shall I, Sir Edward?"

Again that simpering leer into his bored face.

"I greatly treasure my dearest Elaine, but your need is greater than mine, and I therefore relinquish my tenure of her excellent services. My other dear little girls will miss her sorely, but Time heals all wounds. Is that not so, Sir Edward?"

Gruffly, he replied:

"Perhaps, and perhaps not, Mrs. Crane. You will kindly convey my instructions to the young lady as to when she shall accompany me back to my estate? I will bid you good day, Ma'am."

Without another word, he lifted his elbow from the mantelpiece and strode quickly across the floor towards the door. Mrs. Crane fluttered after him, protesting:

"Sir, if you will but wait! One of the servants shall show you out."

I was barely able to contain my delighted amusement. The vision of Mrs. Crane's vast figure puffing in pursuit of the hastily retreating back of the man she plainly considered a gold mine, was almost too much for me. I longed to run forward and slap down those podgy, uplifted arms in their black bombazine sleeves. My mind swiftly compared this behaviour with the normal, day-to-day picture we had of our benefactor: snapping, cruel, unfeeling and hard; yet, where the glitter of gold could be seen, the leopard skulking in the guise of Mrs. Crane speedily changed its spots.

I was not allowed to savour my mirth for long, because I heard the front door clang ominously, followed by the shuffling of angry feet, and then the vast figure filled the doorway. Double chin sunk on heaving bosom, eyebrows meeting like angry darts, and mouth twisted with hate, Mrs. Crane snarled at me:

"I want an explanation of your behaviour, you ungrateful, lazy, good-for-nothing girl! How dare you inveigle yourself into the favour of such a man! How dare you ask him to take you from this place! Have I not cared for you since you were ten? Have I not given you board and lodging, food within your stomach, and clothes to keep the cold from your back? Have I not been both Mother and Father to you these past nine years? Have I not given you an excellent post as teacher of my orphans? How dare you! How *dare* you cheat me out of what by right is mine!"

Her voice had risen to a scream, and I resigned myself to the worst harangue I had received in the recent three years since becoming a teacher in this most dreary of orphanages . . . For The Destitute Children of Gentlefolk.

2

THE final week of my life at the orphanage became a purgatory. Mrs. Crane went out of her way to find fault and to deride me. Nothing I did or touched was correct. Every order was embellished with sneering remarks in which I was being constantly reminded that, had it not been for her own generosity in the matter, I should not be leaving to take up this wonderful new post. It suited Mrs. Crane to forget the donation she had received from Sir Edward Reynauld for this 'privilege', and it was not until many months later that I learned the brutal facts concerning the amount.

My authority in the classroom did not lessen, in spite of the frequent taunts I received before my pupils. They were too frightened of their principal to take any unfair advantage of me. Lessons continued in the normal fashion. Occasionally, I caught one or two envious glances from under puckered brows, and knew that the girls were envying me my good fortune. It was the ambition of each and every one of us to escape the clutches of Mrs. Crane before it was too late.

In some ways, I suppose I had been unfortunate. The children with whom I had grown up had long since left the orphanage; some to domestic service and others to teaching in parish schools. All my life I had realized that these would be the only two paths open to me, yet I had still hoped. I wanted desperately to teach in some quiet home. The prospect of becoming a servant had been too awful to consider. Some households were kind to their minions . . . others were not. However, Mrs. Crane had decided that I was more intelligent than the remainder of my age-group and had chosen my future for me. One morning she had summoned me to her private sitting-room, where I had been informed that I would be taken on as a very junior teacher. Naturally I was to expect no wages at all, because my board and keep would be absorbing every penny. However, as a gracious gesture, she would be prepared to consider a tiny wage at the end of the third year, provided I had given good service.

What could I have replied?

I had agreed to the proposition because I had had no-where else to go. The only alternative would have been domestic service, because I knew Mrs. Crane's recommendation as a private governess would be withheld . . . from spite.

Now, after three years, I was going to be free . . . free!

During the intervening week I had ample opportunity to ponder over my future. What would the child be like? How old was she? Was there more than the one child . . . at school, perhaps? What kind of a man was Sir Edward Reynauld? Had he a large mansion with vast acres of open land The prospect pleased me; I wanted to get away from these high, forbidding walls, from the smells, sights and noise of a busy city, and to go out to the country where solitude abounded.

There were many questions I longed to ask, and I was barely able to contain my impatience until the day came when I could see for myself. I hoped desperately that my new employer would pay another visit to the orphanage to see me, so that we could discuss the future together, but he did not come again. All I succeeded in learning was the date and time of my departure.

My successor was soon chosen and I wanted to weep for her. She was the very epitome of wretched womanhood! Large, terrified eyes stared back from a thin, pallid face, and her frail body looked as if the slightest puff of wind would waft it away. How she would survive the rigours of a cold winter in this cheerless place, I did not know. She rarely spoke and only answered 'yes' or 'no' when addressed.

The night before I left, the pupils came to my room after they had been shut in their dormitory. I trembled with anxiety, terrified that the sharp ears of Mrs. Crane would hear the tell-tale creaking of ancient floorboards as the girls made their stealthy way to my little attic room. I begged them to be careful. Each girl had made a personal gift for me.

Needlecases from scrap materials . . . a posy of useful tape-ends . . . a card of spare buttons scrounged from the bottoms of cupboards, or else retrieved from old clothes, and then sewn on to thin card ... coloured paper jackets for my five precious books ... a tiny bag for hair pins. Any and everything had been put to use and made into something for me as a parting gift.

I was deeply, overwhelmingly touched, because I knew exactly how much care and love had gone into the making of such presents. I knew I should treasure each and every one of them. I still have them all, nestling inside a trinket box bought by my husband in Bodmin a few years ago. He does not laugh at them for their cheapness.

The front door of the Crane Home For Distressed Gentle Orphans closed behind me for the last time at eight-thirty the following morning. Lessons were already well under way, and Mrs. Crane had refused to allow the girls a five minute break in which to bid me farewell. She herself had given me a frosty handshake half an hour previously, advising me to take care that I left with nothing to which I was not entitled ... I was alone.

As I stepped into the open air, I paused to look back at those narrow windows; instead of blankness I could visualize the eleven young heads bent diligently over their slates. Good-bye, my dears! I whispered as I made my way to the heavy gate. May you all have the same good fortune as I!

I carried my few possessions in a small wicker basket, whose handle was threatening to give way. I was thankful, therefore, to see a large coach pulled up outside the entrance. There was a coat-of-arms emblazoned on its fine panelling. I felt a thrill of excitement.

Suddenly the door was thrown open and a voice boomed out:

"Get in, girl! Am I always to be kept waiting?"

My face red, for I had not realized I was unpunctual, I hurried towards the coach. The driver left the head of the lead horse and held out his hand, across which the veins seemed to straggle like the roots of a gigantic tree. His voice was soft.

"I'll take your luggage, Miss."

"Thank you. But it is only the one

little basket." I did not relinquish my hold on its wicker handle, but the driver's hand closed over mine.

"It would be better, Miss, if you don't mind. Sir Edward doesn't like the luggage to travel inside the coach."

"Oh. I understand. Very well, then." I allowed him to take my basket but he must have seen my agitation, for he smiled in a kindly fashion before reassuring me:

"I will take care of it for you, Miss. May I help you climb into the carriage?"

A firm hand lifted my elbow and I was inside the vehicle. The door closed behind me.

"You will sit opposite me," came that deep voice.

"Thank you, Sir."

"I trust most heartily that coach travel does not make you ill?" I blushed.

"I couldn't say, Sir. I haven't travelled in this manner before."

He made a small sound of exasperation, and then turned to look out of the window, a bored expression on his face. I lowered my hands into my lap and fastened my gaze upon them. I longed

26

to reach out and touch the plush satin of the seats, to stroke the fabric with my fingertips. I could not recall the last occasion when such luxury had been within my grasp. I do not know whether Sir Edward had sensed my interest in the upholstery of his travelling coach, because he turned his head towards me, and remarked abruptly:

"Some better quality garments will be found for you on arrival."

My face scorching, I muttered:

"You are too kind, Sir Edward."

"Nonsense! I cannot have my . . . my daughter's governess dressed like a pauper."

He had provided me with the opening I had sought. I leaned slightly forward, my lips parted in eagerness.

"I beg your pardon, Sir, but I know so little about this child. Would you consider it very remiss of me to ask you about her?"

His eyes studied me and, for a fleeting moment, I wondered why their expression seemed to change from disinterest to guarded wariness.

"Ah yes . . . the child." He moved his

legs in front of him as the wheels jolted us over a rough patch of ground. "What is it you wish to know?"

"Her name . . . if you please, Sir. How old she is, and how far she has progressed with her studies."

"Julia," he replied, after a moment's hesitation. "She is . . . ah. Let me think now . . . could it be four? Or five?"

"Oh!" I gasped with surprise. "Then she is indeed little more than a babe."

"Maybe I was mistaken. Six next birthday, perhaps? Yes, that's it."

"Has your wife taught her her letters yet, Sir?"

"Letters? Er . . . no."

I was watching him with eager interest on my face and this expression seemed to annoy him. He waved one hand and said:

"There is plenty of time in which to discuss my Julia. I have answered your questions."

"Thank you, Sir. I did not mean to offend."

He made no response, merely watching the scenery as it passed beyond the window. I leaned against the plush seat-back and thought about our brief, unilluminating conversation.

I decided that his daughter possessed very little interest for him, and that probably he was rather bored with her. I knew this would change as she grew older, becoming more of a companion to him and his wife. I was also thankful that I was to start from the beginning with the child. I had been slightly apprehensive that I might have been a successor to someone else; consequently, I should have been obliged to suffer comparison with my forerunner. I had seen it all so very clearly . . .

The spoiled, unmanageable daughter of a rich land owner, tossing her head in scorn, and telling me:

"Miss Catch-As-Catch-Can didn't teach me to do it *that* way! Are you *quite* certain you've got it right?"

The journey from London was long and tedious, and it necessitated some nights spent at various inns along the way. Sir Edward Reynauld was angry at being obliged to put up at inferior establishments, but I did not care. I was usually so exhausted after a day's travelling that I wanted only to creep up to the tiny attic room they had given me, and to fall on to the straw palliase. I was asleep at once and did not wake until dawn the following morning, when I soon realized that I had shared my bed with many uninvited companions. The irritation from their bites was almost unbearable. I knew I should have to bathe myself completely.

There was no water-jug or basin in my room, so I crept down to the kitchens where I found a slatternly scullion at work near the fire.

"Is there anywhere I can wash?" I asked her politely.

"Wash?" she echoed, staring. "Whatever for?"

A rat scuttled out from the wainscot and she lashed at it with a broom as it brushed past my skirts. On reaching the outer door, it was greeted by delighted barks from the mangy dog which, I suspected, was kept solely to keep down the numbers of such vermin.

"If y'want to wash, there's a bucket by t'well."

"Thank you," I said, and returned to

the bedroom, realizing that my venture had been without success. I needed to take off all my clothes and douse myself completely, but this could not be done in the broad daylight of a busy backyard. I think Sir Edward must have suffered considerably overnight, for we did not travel far on that particular day. When noon arrived, he ordered the coach to be halted at another inn, and then straightway demanded rooms for our use.

It was a pleasant little place, and very clean. The landlord's wife sent a maid to my room with a tub and three buckets of hot water. I bathed myself all over and finished with a brisk hair wash. I then knelt before the fire and dried my long, mousey curls, before fastening them neatly back from my face with hairpins taken from my new hair-pin box. I had just completed my toilet when there came a knock at the door. A servant entered.

"If you please, Miss, His Lordship says you are to dine with him in his rooms."

I put down my comb and thanked the girl. Sir Edward had asked me to share a meal with him! I was excited and grateful. The status of a governess was a somewhat ambiguous one, I had discovered. She was neither equal to her employer, nor lowly enough to consort with the household servants. She was a person aloof, and often she was very lonely because of this. I had always imagined that a paid companion shared similar advantages and disadvantages. It was an honour for one of my kind to be invited to share the master's table. Perhaps Sir Edward wished to discuss his daughter with me?

When I entered the room, I discovered him already at table. He made a slight movement, as if to get up from the table, and then sat down again.

"You're late," he accused. I apologized, and then took my place opposite him. The landlord's wife served me and I started to eat. Nothing more was said for a long time, until Sir Edward suddenly looked up and leaned across the table to me.

"I suppose you are wondering why I sent for you?" he asked, in a gruff voice.

"Yes, Sir. Thank you, Sir."

"Well?"

"Well what, if you please, Sir?" I replied, feeling thoroughly uneasy.

"Aren't you going to ask me why you're here?" he goaded.

"No, Sir. It is not my place to query your motives."

"Quite right, girl. However, I wish to know more about your background. I made a few enquiries from your former employer. What a dragon of a person!"

I could not help smiling at this remark. He caught my amusement and his eyes darkened angrily.

"Are you laughing at my birthmark?" he demanded, his finger smoothing the rough, red flesh.

"Oh no, Sir! It had not occurred to me to notice it more than fleetingly."

"You lie, Madam! Every woman stares at my face. They see this enormous, crescent-shaped mark and wonder." He placed his elbows on the table. "Come now, admit the truth. Had you not wondered about its hideousness?"

I lowered my eyes.

"I will tell you how I came by it,

then your curiosity will be satisfied." He pushed back his chair and rose from the table. I was thankful that the servants had left, for I was acutely embarrassed by this display of self-torment.

"It is the curse of the Reynauld's!" Sir Edward continued, his voice low and intense. "For seven whole generations have we been cursed by this mark." I could not help my exclamation, but would have bitten off my tongue immediately the words had escaped my lips.

"How strange that such things are handed down through the families!"

"There is no mystery about it!" he snarled, and I began to wonder whether he might be a little unbalanced, because his tone implied that I was responsible for the mark upon his countenance. "No mystery at all. It was bequeathed to us. But the women have clear complexions! *They* are not permitted to suffer the stigma of the red crescent!"

I longed for the meal to end so that I could escape the tirade. I muttered a few words of sympathy.

"But you, my dear . . . you will help

me rid the family of this curse!" He had crossed the floor towards me and was now leaning down to stare at me. I felt suddenly very, very afraid.

"Please, Sir, may we . . . talk of your child?" I ventured desperately.

His eyes gazed at me blankly, almost as if the words had passed unheard. Then he shook himself and murmured:

"Ah yes . . . the child . . . my daughter Janet."

"Then you have two girls, Sir?" I asked eagerly.

"Two? What are you talking about?"

"I . . . I thought you said your daughter's name was Julia." I replied meekly. "You meant, I expect, the elder of your children?"

He made no reply but returned to his seat. I was left to puzzle over his words as he rang the bell for the next course. When we had been served, he asked me:

"Were your parents of good stock?" I blushed.

"I hope so, Sir. My father was a sea-captain and my mother a milliner. She was the seventh child in a family of nine; all but two died in infancy. Her brother . . . my uncle Jeremy . . . was killed abroad when I was still very small. My father had no brothers or sisters."

"And your grandparents?"

"All dead, Sir. On the maternal side, they came of genteel, country families, and my father's father was a brave soldier."

"Your mother and father, did they marry for love?"

I thought this a strange question, and frowned across at my employer, wondering why he should concern himself with such irrelevancies.

"It was not arranged by their parents, if that's what you mean, Sir." I replied, a trifle hotly. Then the realization of the implication of the question hit me squarely. I blushed scarlet. Had he the audacity to believe I was the result of some illicit affairs I decided the time had come to meet blunt speaking with further bluntness.

"I am not illegitimate, Sir, if that is your implication."

"Then you are a love-child of a happy marriage."

"I like to consider myself so!" I retorted seethingly, through tight lips. "I wish to protest most strongly against this line of questioning. The exact details of my personal background should be no concern of yours, Sir!"

"I disagree, my dear. Such points are absolutely vital to our future." I made a derisory noise that sounded like a snort. There was no kindness in his expression as he stared at me.

"I suggest, Ma'am, that you return to your room and wait there until the carriage is ready. I intend to travel until well after dark today. We are both refreshed. I will send word when all is prepared."

I pushed aside my plate, cast a regretful glance at the remainder of the compôte of rhubarb, and stood up. Before I left the room, I gave my employer a stiff bow and then registered my disapproval by the rigid set of my back.

As soon as I had reached my room, I began re-packing my meagre possessions. My mind was in a whirl. Had I done right to leave the orphanage? This new assignment seemed to be fraught with all kinds of unanswerable problems, and I had begun to sense fear.

What was I doing here? I wondered, and brushed my hand across my forehead. Is this really happening, or am I having a nightmare? Why had Sir Edward asked me whether I was a love-child?

Suddenly I began to laugh. Of course! How stupid I had been! The answer stared me in the face, only I had been too blind to see it. I did not know very much about my new employer; perhaps he had suffered a great unhappiness during his marriage, resulting in his desire for his small daughter to be schooled and cared for by someone to whom love and affection were not strangers. The more I thought about it, the more convinced I became.

A tremendous surge of relief swept through me, and I longed to meet the little girl.

3

THE rhythmic motion of the carriage tended to lull me to sleep, and this I found most aggravating, because there was so much to be seen from the windows. The countryside bore traces of spring and, the farther west we travelled, the more pronounced became the green freshness of the trees and land. Early wild flowers peeped out at each other from the sheltering tree roots, and new-born lambs skipped and danced in the meadows. I felt a great happiness and longed to reach my new home. It did not matter to me that Sir Edward was silent; I was perfectly happy with my own thoughts. I had drawn a picture in my mind of the little girl whom I was to teach. I gave her large, dark eyes, long chestnut hair that reached to her waist in a cascade of curls, a pretty, cherry-red mouth and a sunny smile. I preferred to forget the sullen twist to her father's lips and the sour expression on his face. I hoped and prayed that his daughter would take more after her mother. Then I began to wonder about this shadowy woman. I was tempted to ask the driver about her, but knew that this could not be done. I must keep my place, I told myself. Later, perhaps, when I had come to know the other servants in the household, then a few questions . . . provided they were not too personal . . . would not come amiss.

Was Lady Reynauld still living? This was a question I dared not voice to my new employer.

It was a mild evening when we drew up in the courtyard of an inn in a tiny village set between steep, green hills. There was just sufficient light left before dusk for me to look out of my bedchamber window at the huddle of neat, thatched cottages with the smoke curling, straight and white, from their stubby chimneys. Hens scratched in the ground around the buildings and, far away, came the deep lowing of cattle. There was a scent in the air which I was unable to trace. Finally I decided it must be the aroma of spring.

There was a knock at the door and a

40

fat, florid-faced woman entered with a jug of hot water and a towel.

"Beg pardon, Miss," she said, "but seeing as how you bain't brought a maid with you, I'll tend to you myself."

"A maid?" I echoed, and then laughed softly. "I am but a servant myself. I'm the new governess!" I declared proudly, although there was no need to explain my presence. The woman's face brightened.

"Oh, in that case, Ma'am, you won't object to a homely body like me waiting on you. From what I'd been told . . . " her voice tailed off and puzzlement returned to her eyes.

"Yes?" I prompted, intrigued. She blushed and lowered her eyes before setting the water-jug beside the empty washbowl.

"'Twere nothing, Miss. I must have made a mistake somehow. This is a busy place, being on the main road, if you see what I mean, and we have lots of travellers eating and resting the night here. I just thought . . . but never you mind, Miss, because it must have been someone else . . . although I could have sworn his man was the same! Still . . . "

she shook her head sadly. "I expect I made a mistake."

"You thought you recognized Sir Edward Reynauld?" I was determined to learn more.

"Yes, but it couldn't have been, seeing as how you're the governess and I'd took you to be the woman he'd gone to London to wed."

I stared at her but she smiled broadly and patted my shoulder.

"Just shows how mistaken one can be, doesn't it? When I learned he'd been to get a wife! Must have mistaken him after all! Now I must get back to the kitchen before those girls make a mess of the dinner. Can't have my guests complaining about my food!"

She hurried from the room and I stared at the whorls of steam which rose from the jug. I thought over our conversation and wondered whether she had been mistaken after all. Everything she had said seemed to fit in so well with my own knowledge of Sir Edward. It was all perfectly simple. It was possible that he had gone to London to fetch his wife; and then, for some reason, she had refused to return with him . . . or else he might have gone to bring home a woman he had been courting, only to have been turned down at the last minute . . . he had set out with intention of restoring a mother. Because he had not wished to disappoint his little girl, he had seized on the opportunity to furnish her with the next best thing . . . a governess. But here he would have come up against a tremendous problem: it was essential to find a woman who was prepared to lavish love on a motherless child . . . hence his choice of myself. He would have known that a girl brought up in the sterility of an orphanage was ideal for his purposes.

I congratulated myself on my swift conjectures and, the more I thought them over, the more convinced I became. It was so easy now to understand the reasons for Sir Edward's off-hand manner and lack of courtesy to myself. He was blistering under the rejection of the woman he loved . . . therefore it was of the greatest importance to him that I should be a love-child!

My prior doubts of him slipped away,

to be replaced with a great sense of compassion. I longed to go to him and say: 'I will give your child the love she craves'; yet I dared not do so, lest he should be angered at my demonstration of pity. Instead, I decided to speak with the coachman, to ask a few simple questions, and to learn more about this child.

My dinner was served in my room and I shall remember it for the rest of my life. After the frugal, ill-cooked fare offered at Mrs. Crane's, this country-style cooking seemed like nectar to a parched tongue. There was roast suckling pig, with its attendant sauces, and roast duckling swimming in a rich gravy, embellished with oranges and apple sauce. These were followed by a huge cake filled with all manners of fruit and spice, and smothered in enormous dollops of a thick, yellowish cream which, the landlady told me proudly, had come from their own cow. I praised her for its quality and confessed that it was the first time in my life that I had partaken of such excellent fare.

"Mercy me!" she cried, raising her

hands. "You have missed a proper treat, Miss."

"Could you please direct me to Sir Edward's coachman?" I asked politely, while I helped her to stack my dirty platters on the tray she had brought.

"Of course, Miss. If you don't object to coming into my kitchen. I assure you, you'll find little to criticize because my good man and I like to keep a clean and wholesome table for our guests."

"I'm sure I won't, Ma'am," I responded, and then held the door, before following her down the dark staircase to the narrow passage which led to the servants' quarters. I was not certain which rooms had been allotted to Sir Edward, and hoped he would not decide to come on to the landing as I was passing. To my relief, all the doors remained tightly shut.

I found the coachman sitting at the scrubbed table which stood in the centre of a vast kitchen. Hams, salted meats, strings of vegetables and bunches of dried herbs hung in tidy rows from thick beams set into the high ceiling. Over the fire, a soot-blackened pot was suspended from a chain, while beside it lay a panting mongrel, not long since released from the spit-wheel that was built into the stone fireplace.

"The young lady wished to speak with you, Mr. Parker," the landlord's wife said, addressing the coachman. His mouth was full, and he hastened to swallow before standing up and touching his forelock.

"I be at your service, Miss."

"I'd like a few words with you alone, if I may."

"Is something wrong, Miss?" The man was plainly ill at ease, and I began to wonder whether I had done right to come seeking him. I nodded.

"If it's all the same with you, Miss, we'll go back into the passage, me not liking to disturb those whose rightful place it is to be in here." He came round the table and held the door for me. I waited in the passage while he fastened the catch, and we were alone together. He glanced into the gloom and said in a hushed voice:

"Beg pardon, Miss, but do the Master know you're here?"

"No. Mr. Parker, he doesn't."

"I be only Parker to you, Miss," he pointed out. "I be only the coachman and stablehand when we back at the house." He cast another furtive glance up the passage. "You quite certain the Master don't know you're with me?"

I was beginning to lose patience.

"Of course he doesn't. I simply wanted to ask you a few questions. Surely there can be no harm in that? If you don't approve, then I'll go to Sir Edward direct, although I fear I shall embarrass him."

"You do what you think fit, Miss," Parker advised in a slow tone. "Bain't my place to tell nothing."

I laughed impatiently as I scolded:

"Come now, Parker! I just want to ask you about Miss Julia."

He seemed to shrink against the wall.

"Oh no, Miss! None of us talks of Miss Julia now!"

"Why ever not? If I'm to teach the child, surely I'm entitled to find out about her?"

"Child, Miss?"

I was fast losing my temper at the old man's imbecility.

"Who else, man?" I retorted, rather snappishly. "Sir Edward's daughter, Julia; who, I believe, is five or six years of age." I saw Parker's head move in the darkness.

"No, Miss, you got it wrong. There bain't no daughter. Sir Edward bain't got no babbies and, if that's what you be coming to Cornwall for, then you get off home, quick. Afore 'tis too late."

I recoiled.

"I . . . I don't understand!" I protested. "I'm to be governess to his little girl!" I was beginning to wonder if Parker was more simple than he appeared. "Then who . . . who is Julia?" My voice was toneless.

"Sir Edward's first wife, Miss."

Weakly, I added:

"And Janet?"

"That were his second wife, Miss. Only we bain't allowed to mention them, seeing as how they're both dead and buried."

"Then . . . then *why* am I to be employed as governess? Parker, are you *sure* you're telling me the truth? Perhaps there is another little girl living in the house?" I asked wildly, my head buzzing.

"No, Miss. There bain't been no babbies in Reynauld House since the present Master were a lad. And a proper wicked devil he was too, Miss!" He lifted his hand to scratch his head. "Beg pardon, Miss, but if you don't know the truth, then why did you come?"

"I'm sorry. I still don't understand what you mean."

"'Tis like this, Miss. Master said he were going to Lunnon to bring home a new wife. He has to, you see, because he be the last of the line, and he's . . . never mind, Miss. I takes a little while to sort things out, not being blessed with a quick brain like other folks. Master said he'd go to Lunnon and choose the new mistress, then everything would be all right again. When he fetched you, I thought you knew all about it."

I leaned against the stone wall and rubbed an arm across my sweating brow. The enormity of my position hit me like a gigantic blow.

"You mean . . . *I* am to become the third Lady Reynauld?"

"That be it, I reckon. Only it don't

seem right now, do it, with you not knowing about it! Now I know why Master didn't want me to speak to you, just in case I lets the rats out of the trap."

"But he can't *force* me to marry him against my will!" I protested, laughing in a strained fashion. "He has to have my consent."

"That's as maybe, Miss, but you don't know the Master when he sets his mind on something. He's got to marry someone."

"Why?" I snapped.

"'Tis all he's got left to do if he wants to break the curse."

"Curse?" I almost shouted. "What is all this? Some kind of stupid nightmare, or a figment of your own imagination?"

"You be right to accuse me, Miss," he replied sorrowfully. "But I'm not all that slow or simple. The curse of the Reynaulds is a very real matter, and like as not you'll be finding out about it when you be wed to the Master."

"I will *not* marry a man I don't even like!" I gripped both his arms. "Listen! You've got to help me. I must get away from here as soon as possible."

"But where would you go, Miss? Do you know these parts at all?"

"No, but someone will help me, I'm sure."

"I don't know nobody neither."

"Then you'll help me?" I begged, shaking him in my anxiety.

"I daren't, Miss."

"What do you mean?" I demanded with anger. "Why can't you help me get away?"

"If the Master finds out what I done, he'll . . . he'll . . . oh, Miss I *wish* I could help you, but I just can't." There was genuine contrition in his voice and my anger subsided.

"Tell me about it," I suggested, a little more kindly this time.

"You see, Miss, it be my old mother. We been living in a cottage on the estate all our lives; then I wanted to find employment elsewhere and the Master said I wasn't to go. I only wanted to work in the tin mine back along three miles, but he told me that if I left he'd turn us both out of the cottage. Not that he wanted it for anyone else, Miss; it

were just his way of doing things. So I
didn't dare leave." He paused to wipe
his sleeve across his upper lip, then he
sniffed. "Other times, when I didn't seem
too happy at some of the things he told
me to do . . . like setting fire to old
widow Buse's furniture when she passed
over . . . "

"Surely that was a sensible act if she
was alone in the world?"

"But she weren't, Miss! That was the
trouble. Because she had a young maid
. . . plain as a pikestaff and with a twisted
leg . . . none of the lads wanted her in
marriage and she couldn't earn much
. . . he turned her out of her home and
burned all her things."

"How very dreadful!"

"It weren't very nice, Miss, but the
Master's word is law in the village. Poor
little Annie walked into the sea, twisted
leg and all, because there was nothing
left. She didn't wait for us to help.
Just went and drowned herself. I didn't
like burning her things while she were
looking on. Tears streaking her plain
little face, and her shoulders shaking
with grief; only she bain't be making

any sound, and that was the awful part of it, Miss. So you see, Miss, if I don't do as I be told, then the Master will turn my mother out of her home. She's too old for work and almost blind, having spent the better part of her working life toiling in the dark rooms up at the House mending the linen for the Master's father. And he were just the same kind of devil, too! Can't get away from it because 'tis part of the curse, you see, Miss. I'd like to help you, but I daren't."

"Have you any suggestion as to where I might go?" I asked gently, my own plight fading into insignificance beside his story.

"Have you any money, Miss?"

"They didn't pay me at the orphanage."

His face turned towards me as he murmured sympathetically:

"Poor maid! Then 'twouldn't be no good your going back there."

"No. Sir Edward might come looking for me."

"They be good folk here in Devon," Parker commented. "If you was to run off and hide for the night until we go on again in the morning, then I reckon you could soon find someone willing to take you on. Can you cook?"

"Yes. And I'm used to hard toil. I'll do anything, as long as I can get away from Sir Edward."

"'Twouldn't do for you to hide in the village here, because Master will search everywhere for you. Best plan is to slip out and run as far as you can get on to the moorland proper! 'Tis an absolute death-trap, specially in the dark. You find a nice wood and hide under the bushes. You'll be safe there. Here," he dipped his hand into a pocket and then I felt the coldness of a coin as he pressed it into my palm. "Take this. You'll not be without food. I bain't be able to help you any other way, but my dear mother would never forgive me if she knew I'd turned you away without a halfpenny."

"Are you sure you'll be all right?" I asked him anxiously. The fact that I had no money did not bother me nearly as much as the possible retribution against this kindly, generous man.

"I won't tell, and neither will you. I daren't take food from the kitchen, because the landlord bain't done nothing against the Master. The Missis would probably give you something, but 'tis better she don't know nothing at all, then the Master can't punish her in any way. You take my money, Miss, and buy something on the way. Have you a warm shawl to put about your shoulders?" His hands had slipped up my arms and were touching my back. "You seem a mite thin and delicate," he finished sadly. "'Tis cold and bitter at night on the moors and I wouldn't be wanting to think of you dying of cold."

In spite of myself and the predicament in which I had found myself, I managed to laugh.

"You'd be surprised how strong I am, Parker! Years of working in un-heated rooms have toughened me. If I can survive winters when icicles form at the tip of my nose, and my fingers turn stiff and purple, then I'm sure I can face the rigours of a Devonshire moorland."

"I wish you luck, Miss." He gripped my hand and squeezed it hard. "Go as soon as you can."

"I had better wait until everyone has gone to bed," I suggested, having considered the possibility that Sir Edward might take it into his head to summon me before settling down for the night.

"You do that, Miss. Can you climb out of your window, or do you have to come downstairs? They've got big dogs in there." He jerked his head in the direction of the kitchen behind us.

I recalled the minutes I had spent looking out of my window at the village. Surely there had been a gently sloping roof a couple of feet below? Could I climb out on to it and then lower myself to the ground beneath?

I told Parker what I had seen.

"Tell you what, Miss. You go back into your room and carry the candle to the window, while I go into the courtyard to see how far you have to fall. Then I'll know your window."

I thanked him for his kindness, but begged him to take care, because I was not certain whether Sir Edward's window overlooked the same portion of courtyard as my own. Then I crept back upstairs. I did as Parker had suggested and heard a faint whistle from beneath the window.

"Yes?" My voice was barely audible.

Parker vanished from sight and then I saw his hand reaching over the edge of the roof and clasping it. It remained there for a moment, then his face reappeared.

"Thank you!" I called softly. He waved and then went back indoors. I felt a surge of enormous relief. Getting away from the inn presented me with little difficulty, because a swift appraisal of Parker's height had shown me that the roof was barely six feet from the ground. By hanging from it with my hands, my own feet would probably be about six or seven inches off the stone of the courtyard.

I placed the candle on the table and found one of my books. Then I settled down to wait until the time arrived for me to pretend to go to bed.

4

THE candle spluttered in a fitful draught from my window and I drew my feet under my body because I was chilled. Would the landlord ever go to bed? I wondered as I heard sounds of movement from downstairs. Dishes clattered, a dog barked once, and then came the welcoming whinny of a horse when someone went into the stable at the far side of the courtyard.

Everything was ready. I had given up trying to read over an hour beforehand, and had tucked my book into my small bag for when I should flee. I had no idea of the time, but guessed that it was late, because the thin sickle moon had travelled a fair distance across the area of my window since I had spoken to Parker.

I pulled my shawl about my body and waited.

The noises died away, then there came the sound of heavy feet tramping up a flight of stairs somewhere in the distance, and I knew that the landlord had retired to bed at last. Cautiously I rose to my feet and the floor-boards creaked ominously. I gasped, and waited. Then I chided myself for an unnecessary fear: at night, all floors and timbers creaked in older houses. Mrs. Crane's orphanage had had its share of nocturnal sounds, although we often laughed girlishly amongst ourselves, saying that the building did not dare to protest *too* much, for fear of Mrs. Crane's displeasure.

I went to the window and opened it fully. The air outside held a chill and I shivered, but I think excitement must have caused most of my trembling. I leaned out and inspected the windows along the wall. All were in darkness. It was safe to start on my lone journey. I went back into the room, collected my bag and swung it over my arm. Then I blew out the candle and paused in the darkness until my eyes had become accommodated to the gloom. The window waited in front of me like a giant grey rectangle, and only my determination to get away from Sir

Edward drove me towards it, helped me swing my legs out and over, and then turn on to my stomach. The bag bumped noisily and my breath seemed to suffocate me. I slithered and scraped my way down the roof, my hands holding tightly to the window sill. I wondered wildly if my feet would reach the edge and suddenly they were there!

I tucked my toes over the edge, feeling for a gutter, but there was none. All I had to do was to let go slowly and allow myself to glide gently into the black void beneath.

First one hand . . .

Then the other . . .

I felt such a ninny, because I could not move! The slope of the roof was too gentle to allow the weight of my body to take me over the edge. I began to push warily with my hands, elbows bent, and my legs protruded beyond the roof. I felt bruised as the rough tiles beneath dug into me, but I continued to propel myself nearer . . . nearer that sheer drop.

Suddenly I bent my legs and the lower portion of my body overhung the roof, rather like a sack. Its weight increased the rate of my descent and my palms were being ripped as I started to slide at speed. I bit back a cry and wondered, terrified, if I should fall on to my back on the ground.

My fingernails met the sharp edge of the roof and I tightened my grip with all the strength I possessed. The bag over my arm swung to and fro, beating my face and neck. My legs dangled and swung while I steadied myself. Then, very carefully indeed, I bent my knees and let go with my hands.

The ground seemed to rush up to meet me, stinging the soles of my feet in the well-worn fabric of my serviceable boots (kindly provided by courtesy of the Crane Home) and I tipped over on to my posterior. Within seconds, I was scrambling to my feet again; conscious, however, of a sharp pain in my right ankle where I must have sprained it on landing.

I would not give in now! I decided determinedly. I could not even afford to rest in order to ease the hurt, because a dog had started to bark within the kitchens. I limped across the courtyard, trusting to instinct that I was heading in the right direction.

I fumbled with the catch on the gate that I had suddenly discovered in front of me, and wondered what on earth I thought I was doing! Searching my memory, I had no recollection of a gate when we had arrived earlier that evening. I moved away from it, feeling with my hands first its timbers, then a stone wall, and suddenly . . . welcome emptiness!

I heaved a sigh of relief and realized what I must have done. The landlord had a private garden, guarded by a wicket gate, and it had been this that I had stumbled against. The emptiness before me was the entrance to the main street which ran outside. I wished I had more time in which to wait, but I dared not do so, for the dog was still barking as if to warn its master that all was not well within the precincts of his tavern.

The road was rough and pitted, obliging me to make my way with care. The trees and other dwellings stood out against the sky as grey against darker grey. A candle flickered in the window of one cottage about twenty yards ahead of me and, as I approached, I caught the sound of a child's fretful cry. I smiled. They would not hear my passage, I thought.

Direction was immaterial to me. As long as I put as much distance between Sir Edward Reynauld and myself was all that concerned me. I had to leave the main road at the earliest opportunity and take to the open countryside. I did not believe that any form of pursuit was likely until daylight the following morning, but this was no excuse for complacency. Every step I took meant a further degree of safety.

I paused to regain my breath and to ease the ache in my ankle. I looked back along the way I had come, but there were no lights to distinguish the village from the remainder of the countryside. I felt sure I would have been seen had the innkeeper been roused to activity by his vigilant hound. Then I peered along the road in front of me, trying to decide whether this was the road by which we had travelled, or the one to be taken in continuance of the journey. Had the inn been on my left or my right from the carriage? On my left . . . but had we swung in a complete circle to reach the courtyard, or had it been a straight, direct approach?

I decided not to bother my brain with trivialities now, and to find an open field as quickly as I could. The road down which I now hurried was hedged by thick bushes and trees. Was there a wood close by? And how to reach the open moorland? Surely I must have been walking uphill for the past five minutes?

Oh dear, the darkness of the night is *so* deceptive!

Within minutes, the long line of bushes came to an end and I was able to take a sharp turn to the left, and strike out across the open country. This was much better! Then I felt a breeze on my face and a steepening of the terrain. A thrill shot through me. I was leaving the valley in which lay the village! Soon . . . soon.

The uphill stretch seemed interminable. When I had reached the flat, undulating summit, I paused to catch my breath. I wanted to sit down and rest my ankle but knew that this would be very dangerous. Once I had eased it I should not want to continue, and I felt quite sure that I was not even a mile away from the village. I *had* to go on . . . and on . . . and on!

It was easier now that my progress was downhill but all too soon the ground tilted upwards again, and I was bent almost double as I toiled up a steep slope. What kind of land was this? I asked myself angrily. First gentle, and now vicious in its shape. Had I strayed towards a mountain? I paused to lean back, my hands on my hips, and to search the night for the summit. There it was, not far from me, yet seemingly very, very high.

Somehow I reached it and, to my joy, found myself at the edge of a deep expanse of woodland, as I discovered on making my way through it. When I had walked about a hundred yards, I sat down and leaned against a tree trunk to rest my aching limbs, and to ease the red hot throbbing of my ankle. I lost account of the time I spent there; although I do not believe it could have been over long. When I stood up again, and rested my weight upon the injured leg, fierce pains shot through me and I gasped loudly. I paused, and then tested my weight once more. This time the pain was not quite so harsh. I took another step, then another. Soon the pain had receded to a dull glow and I pretended to forget it completely. I knew, however, that I must not allow myself to sit down, lest I should be unable to rise at all.

It was easier to walk now because the ground was flat. I set out gamely and walked at a firm, steady rate, counting quietly to myself. I threaded my way through the trees, groping in front of me with my hands, lest I should walk headlong into one of stalwart, immobile monsters with their lichen overcoats. Around me I could hear the busy scurry and scamper of night creatures, while above my head the branches whispered and clattered against each other. All sound was suspended at the sudden 'hoo, hoo' of a marauding owl.

I lost track of time and distance. It seemed that this wood was endless. I staggered and almost fell, longing to collapse on to the ground and fall into a deep, dreamless sleep. The fear of Sir Edward receded into the past like the awakening from some ghastly nightmare.

It was all a dream . . . a bad dream from which I shall soon awake, I told myself.

I paused and tried opening my eyes wide: a practice I had cultivated as a young child when realizing that the dream in which I moved was unpleasant. If I tried hard enough, I was always able to wake myself up, although the effort of keeping my eyes open until I had shaken my head free of the dream had often proved too much; thereby dropping me straight back into the terror once more. This time, however, I knew I was not dreaming, and my strenuous eye-efforts were useless.

I stood still, listening.

I wanted to laugh aloud. From my right came the welcome tinkle of a stream. I would reach it and sit on its banks, bathing my injured ankle in its coolness. I turned in its direction and staggered on. Then I paused, blinking, and almost unable to believe my eyes. In front of me, a clearing had opened up and a fire was glowing in its centre.

I almost ran to the fire, oblivious to the fact that where there were flames, there must be people . . .

A dog whined . . .

I reached the fire and bent over its dim redness, rubbing my hands together. Then I sank down on to the ground as a wave of faintness swept over me. The stream began to roar like a torrent in my ears and I knew no more.

When I reopened my eyes, I found myself gazing up at the light patch of sky between the trees and it seemed to me that dawn had arrived. Then a darker silhouette moved between me and the sky, and I saw a man's head.

Another head, over to the right . . . I twisted my own slightly to look up at it. A voice muttered in a language I did not understand.

I tried to sit up and a firm hand restrained me while a voice said, in English this time:

"You are hurt?"

"I . . . my foot," I replied weakly.

"Jocasta!"

The second head blocked out the sky and I caught the dangling of a large ear-ring below a scarfed face. The voice continued speaking in the strange tongue, then added to me:

"Which leg?"

I lifted it and gentle fingers prodded the swollen ankle.

"Can you walk?"

"I think so."

"Then you must go to Jocasta's wagon where she will anoint and wrap your ankle. Let me take your hand."

A strong arm came round my shoulders and I was almost lifted from the ground. The man laughed near my ear.

"You are so little! It is good you came to us. So easy to be lost in these woods."

I leaned against his supporting body, surprised at the exhaustion I now felt. We left the fire and went towards a large cart which stood on the edge of the clearing. The woman who had been leaning over me was already inside. busying herself with jars and cloths. A small girl almost tumbled down the steps in her haste to fill a tin basin with water from the pail that hung on a hook below the tailboard.

"In here, Miss. Jocasta will care for you. Then you will eat."

He helped me up the steps and I sank

on to a bunk just inside the covered cart. He remained outside and the rapidly improving dawn light illuminated his cheerful face. His skin was dark and swarthy; eyes piercing, and teeth bad. I saw, too, that he wore one ear-ring, rather like a buccaneer.

"Are you gipsies?" I ventured at last, while Jocasta bathed my swollen ankle.

"Romany folk," came his reply. "It is good you came to us. You were lost in the night, perhaps?"

I shook my head.

"I have run away from a bad man."

He tut-tutted sadly.

"Your father, perhaps? It is bad. But we will help you. Where do you want to go?"

"I'm not sure." I told him doubtfully. "I do not know this part of the country at all."

"Where have you come from?"

"London."

"No. I mean, which place near here?"

"I'm sorry. I can't tell you. It was very nearly dark by the time we reached the village. I didn't think to ask its name."

"Village? Let me think. Could be . . . "

he mused, stroking his chin. "Have you walked long tonight?"

"Hours and hours!" I exclaimed. Then I laughed.

He mentioned the name of a village.

"Could it have been that one, perhaps? But it is not far away from here. Unless . . . unless . . . " There was doubt and concern in his tone. I reached out to grip his arm.

"Please tell me!" I begged. "What is wrong?"

"The village lies just beyond the hill. You may have walked round in a circle, perhaps. Or it may have been for many, many miles that you have come."

I described the village to him, and his face became solemn.

"It is sad," he commented carefully, almost as if he did not wish to fill me with despair, "very, very sad that you could not see the way in the wood. You have travelled many miles and are now back where you started."

I burst into tears. Everything seemed so fruitless. Why had I not thought of this possibility? I chided myself. So much effort, pain, and time wasted, while all I had been doing was to walk in a huge circle.

I felt Jocasta's hand on my knee as she completed winding a bandage about my ankle. Then she started to speak in a rapid flow.

"My Jocasta say we will help you to a good town. Never fear."

"Thank you! Thank you!" I wept.

"It was well we remained here one more night," the man continued: "The little one, Linnet, was ill in the morning yesterday, so we did not go with the other Romany folk. They started in the morning and we would follow when little Linnet's sickness had passed. As you see, she is quite well again and we can rejoin our great big family!" He beamed at me and then ruffled his daughter's hair affectionately. She grinned with shyness and I could see that she had lost her front milk teeth.

"You rest while Jocasta and I find food for you."

I shall never forget the kindness of those Romany folk. Although poor, their generosity towards me seemed boundless. I told them that I should be quite all right on my own, but they refused to listen. They would take me eastwards towards Exeter where I would be safe from pursuit. They waited on me, even though I said that my ankle was better, but Jocasta simply pushed me back on to the bunk and brought me my share of food in an earthenware bowl. The child, Linnet, settled herself beside me and watched while I ate. When I lifted a mouthful to my lips, so did she. We had no knives or other cutlery: fingers were our natural tools.

The sun had risen and the birds in the woods were singing and calling to one another.

"It will be a good day for travelling," the man told me, grinning. "The mule has eaten, also the dog, and we will start on our way to the east."

I breathed a sigh of relief, because I knew that each mile we took in an easterly direction would bear me further from Sir Edward Reynauld.

But my relief was premature.

The mule had been backed between the shafts where Linnet was helping her father fasten the harness; Jocasta was putting away her scoured cooking pots, and I was savouring the last morsel of hard, oatmeal biscuit, when the sounds came to us. With one accord, our heads turned towards the trees, listening.

Twigs snapped, hooves thundered, and a voice called out:

"Whoa!"

Sir Edward Reynauld rode into the clearing and pulled rein with such force that his horse reared. I leaned back against the inside of the wagon, hoping the interior gloom would hide me from view. I saw Sir Edward swing himself down from the saddle, toss the reins over a thin branch, and come striding across to the gipsy who had returned to his job of harnessing the mule. Linnet ducked under the animal's belly and rushed across to the wagon, sprinting up the steps as if a wild bull were in pursuit. She thrust her arms around her mother's waist and then stood with her at the entrance to the wagon; thereby effectively hiding me from outside view. I could hear Sir Edward's voice demanding to know if my presence had been noticed, and in which direction I had been bound.

I waited anxiously for the gipsy's reply, but he said nothing.

"Come. She is here," he said, at last.

I simply could not believe my ears! After all his promises of help, my new friend had turned traitor to me. I stared at Jocasta who was edging into the front of the wagon, stark terror on her face.

"What is wrong now?" I asked.

She pointed wildly with one hand and then clutched her child to her, babbling in the language I was unable to understand. I felt deeply frustrated.

"I will pay gold," Sir Edward was saying as the two men approached the wagon. I stood up and went to the steps. The sun shone on me.

"I will touch no tainted money!" I heard the gipsy's snarl as he came up the steps towards me. I was unable to hide my bitter disappointment.

"Why have you betrayed me?" I asked softly.

"Child," he replied, "I am powerless to help you now. You must go with this man."

"Even though it will mean misery and

despair?" I almost shouted at him. His face was sad.

"If you stay it will bring death not only to yourself, but also to me and my beloved ones."

"Death?" I echoed, uncomprehending these strange words.

"Death." He swung round and his right arm shot out, the forefinger extended towards the livid mark on Sir Edward's face. "Do you see the crescent? He has been cursed by one of my own race. He bears the Romany mark of hate. We are all powerless against it, and to help you will bring disaster to all of us."

I was quite bewildered. Sir Edward had flushed and was now fingering the birthmark on his cheek. He looked up at me and his eyes hardened.

"Come, Miss Salt. We have things to do."

I felt the gipsy's body close behind me, and then something was slipped into my hand. My fingers closed over it, and I then tucked it into a fold in my skirt. His wife's eyes had not missed the movement and she smiled at me.

"We cannot help you, but we can

protect you once you are away from us. Wear the charm . . . always." His voice was a low whisper.

"Here is gold!" Sir Edward snapped, tossing a coin on to the ground in front of the steps. With expert aim, the gipsy spat on the shining guinea piece.

"It shall lie where it has fallen," he said, offering me his hand while I came gingerly down the wagon steps.

"You have been very kind," I said, pressing his hand when I had reached the ground. "I do not blame you for turning me away. Later, I may learn about the evil that surrounds my employer."

Sir Edward was growing impatient. He seized me by the waist and lifted me into the saddle, then he swung himself up behind me. I shuddered as his arms went round me from behind. His hands closed over the reins. The feel of his body against mine was alien and unpleasant. I was frightened by its evil power.

"You will not elude me again, my dear," he promised confidently as we turned away from the gipsy encampment. "I should have suspected you would try such a trick. Who helped you?"

"No one," I responded quickly. "It was easy to leave my room. You can't force me to go with you!" I declared, with sudden boldness. "When we get back to the inn I'll make a fuss and refuse to leave with you."

His only answer was a low laugh. I saw the reason for his mirth when we rode out of the wood. There, waiting for us in the road, stood Sir Edward's carriage. A stable lad hovered anxiously beside Parker, who glanced sheepishly at me, as if he wanted to convey that he had not informed his master of my hasty departure. Conscious of the latter's keen scrutiny, I pretended disinterest in Parker, and soon sensed his relief.

"Can I take the mare back to the inn now, Sir?" the stable lad asked when Sir Edward had dismounted and was helping me down.

"Of course. We shall be on our way now."

Then I was assisted into the carriage and the door shut on us both. I was reminded forcibly of the clanging of a grille in a prison cell.

5

MY ankle was propped up on the seat while my head rested wearily against the side window, jerking and bouncing as the horses covered the uneven ground. I was in the depths of despair and knew that Sir Edward was watching me.

"Why did you bring me back?" I asked dully. "I am not the wife for you."

"Then you heard the tale?" he asked, and I nodded.

"The innkeeper's wife told me."

"I should have expected as much. Still, no real harm done. You were bound to learn the truth sooner or later."

"There was no need for deceit," I pointed out, rather stupidly, for he laughed.

"Would you have agreed to come with me had you known?"

"Of course not. I refuse to marry where I don't even love."

"You are forgetting, my dear, that I *paid* for you!"

My stomach seemed to curl up into a tight, strangling ball.

"Paid?" I echoed.

"Naturally. You didn't expect the revered Mrs. Crane to give away her cherished teacher without some suitable reimbursement, did you?" He chuckled. "I have paid a fairly high price for your . . . er . . . services, Miss Salt, and I do not intend my money to be wasted."

"You fiend!"

"I bought you and it is my intention that you will repay me fully by producing a son and heir to the family name."

The cold manner in which he was discussing this matter of delicacy was quite unbelievable. I felt my face redden in embarrassment, then he leaned over to touch my lap. I shuddered uncontrollably.

"Yes, my dear. I wish most desperately for a son and, when I first set eyes on you walking with those girls, I knew my quest for a wife had come to an end. If you had but known the lengths to which I have been to procure someone as eminently suitable as yourself!" He sighed. "I was

80

beginning to despair after so many long, fruitless weeks. Then chance directed my feet towards the orphanage and I knew I should triumph."

"You can't make me!" I blustered.

"Make you do what, my dear?" he continued in a silky voice.

"Marry you, of course!"

"How will you stop me, pray? And to whom are you thinking of running? You have no home, no friends, and I am quite certain Mrs. Crane would not have you back."

"I should have told her of your perfidy!" I retorted.

"But would she have believed you, I wonder? The arrangement between us was purely a business agreement. She was paid handsomely for your services . . . as a governess, don't forget! As soon as you turned up on her doorstep, she'd have sent you packing post haste; for fear that I would be demanding the return of my money, I regret to say, and not for any other altruistic reason."

"But you still can't *make* me marry you!" I told him with bright confidence. "The bride's permission has to be given during the actual service."

"And you will be giving it, never fret."

"I most certainly will *not*!"

He began to laugh, and then turned away his face to look out of the window, leaving me with the feeling that he had bested me in some manner I had not been able to comprehend. I racked my brains, trying to find some further avenue of escape.

"What about the gipsy's curse?" I demanded, my tone harsh in the sudden silence between us.

"It is immaterial to you," came the deft, bored response. "No doubt one of the family retainers will feel it to be his or her duty to enlighten you on the facts. Cannot you wait until then?"

"I want to get out!" I insisted in sudden panic. I swung my legs on to the floor and winced at the pain. His eyes caught my expression and he smiled.

"I think you'll stay there as long as is necessary."

With a disdainful sniff I looked away, but did not put my aching leg back on to the seat for a further five minutes. I suppose I wanted to show him that I could be just as stubborn as he was.

We passed very little traffic on the road, and the plan I had formulated for slamming down the window and calling out to other vehicles that I was being abducted, faded. But I still clung desperately to the hope that I could not be forced to marry this man against my will. I would throw myself at the mercy of the clergyman and he would have only the one course to follow . . .

Two hours passed and no further words were exchanged between us. My mind was busy planning what I should do when we stopped at an inn for a meal. No, Sir Edward could *not* force me to remain with him! I thought, with triumph. I would cause such a commotion of shouting and screaming, begging for help from those around me, that a constable would be sent for from the parish and my safety ensured. My spirits rose again.

I do not know whether my triumph showed in my expression, but I ought to have been warned by Sir Edward's silence. Had I known him better, I would not have presumed such confidence in my ultimate success. Oh, the foolish pride of inexperience!

Sir Edward moved in his seat and tapped hard with his silver-topped cane at the roof of the vehicle. Parker pulled up and I could hear the horses snorting and pawing the ground. The door opened.

"Sir?"

"Bring in the hamper, Parker. We will eat now."

I bit back my disappointment. The thought had not occurred to me that this man would have made arrangements back at the inn for a packed meal. I comforted myself with the thought that all was by no means lost. We still had to sleep at night and rest the horses.

The hamper was brought down from its place under Parker's seat and Sir Edward opened it.

"Let us see what mine host has provided," he said lifting out a clean white cloth and laying it carefully on the scat beside him. "Parker, bring the wine."

"The wine, Sir?"

"The bottle I gave you this morning."

"Yes, Sir." He left us and returned almost immediately with a dark green bottle.

The sight of cold roast chicken, slices of cold beef, pies and pastries made my mouth water. I knew it would take me some time to become accustomed to luxurious fare after the frugal and dreary diet of the orphanage. Sir Edward saw my interest and a smile hovered at the corners of his mouth.

"You will take a glass of ratafia?" he asked, taking up a glass and unstoppering the bottle in his left hand.

"I . . . " I began to protest, but he swiftly silenced me.

"You will drink this. The wine will ease your ankle." If any words would entice me to drink, these were they. It was essential that I should rid myself of pain if I wanted to effect a good escape later in the day. I held out my hand for the glass and raised it to my lips. Then I grimaced, for its taste was bitter.

"It is good, yes?" my companion asked, and his dark eyes gleamed with something I only recognized when it was too late . . . triumph.

"Yes," I replied, determined he should not witness my distaste. He continued to watch me as I took another sip. The fiery liquid made me feel as if I would choke, but I steeled myself to drink calmly.

The level of the ratafia was now half-way down the glass. I looked at it and suddenly it seemed to take on the appearance of a deep, dark pool. I raised my eyes and noticed that a haze now enveloped everything around me. Then my head began to throb and I knew with an awful intensity that I had been tricked. The glass tipped over in my hand, spilling its contents on to my travelling cloak.

"I . . . you . . . you . . . " the words would not come. My throat felt as if it were paralysed. I had been drugged! Vaguely I heard the shattering of glass as the vessel reached the floor, and then I fell back against the seat. I saw Sir Edward rise and come towards me, his arms outstretched. I wanted to scream with fear when he bent over me. My eyes must have shown him my terror, for I heard him say, as if from a great distance:

"It is too late. I have won."

The haze thickened and became black. I tried to lift my hands to push him away, and the last thing I knew was the soft warmth of a rug which he tucked around me.

★ ★ ★

I cannot recall everything that happened after I had drunk of that hateful liquid. I dimly remember the jolting of the carriage, the uselessness of my limbs and strong arms about me when I was lifted from the vehicle and carried into some form of dwelling-place. I tried to call out, but was unable to mouth the words. I heard Sir Edward's voice tell someone:

"She is extremely unwell. Your best room, at once!"

Then there was softness beneath me and a woman's hands about me while I felt my clothes being removed. I could barely keep my eyes open and I tried to grip her arms, but she pushed me gently back, saying:

"There my pretty! You bide here awhile and sleep."

Help me! Help me! Help me! The words rang inside my head but left my mouth only as a harsh croak.

Then her arms came about me again and I felt her lift me from the pillows. In her right hand, she held a glass and I heard a scream of terror within my head.

No! No! No! It is drugged! I shouted.

"Drink this, my pretty, then you'll feel better."

I tried to push away the glass. I tried to twist myself off the bed. I tried to shout and cry. But I could not. I felt as if enormous weights had pinned me to that bed. The glass came closer. It touched my lips. I felt liquid within my mouth and the sensation it left when it slid down my throat against my will. I tried to retch, but even this was denied me.

"Now you must sleep, my pretty," I heard the woman say, and darkness swept over me like a blanket.

When next I opened my eyes it was to see Sir Edward sitting by the bed. My head seemed clearer and I found that I was able to use my hands to pull the bedclothes about my neck. He noticed this movement and nodded. Then his hand moved to the bedside table and I saw him pick up a decanter, from which he filled a glass and held it in front of me.

"No! Please no!" I whispered.

"That is better," he said, replacing the glass. "Are you prepared to listen to what I have to say, or are you determined to keep up this infantile resistance? It can do you no good, you know."

I said nothing, turning my face to the pillow so that he should not see the tears which had come to my eyes.

"I wish to marry," my captor continued in a calm voice. "It is immaterial to me whether you are agreeable. You come of good stock, have a healthy body, and should provide me easily with the heir I need. I have arranged for a priest to come here and marry us."

I turned to look at him and he nodded.

"Yes, my dear. He should be here within the hour. I have two courses open to me. First, you will marry me without protest and nothing will happen to the reverend gentleman; or, should you still prove difficult, I shall force some more of this wine," he held up the glass so that I should not mistake his meaning, "this wine upon you. After which, the reverend gentleman will not find his way home in safety."

"What . . . what do you mean?" I asked, puzzled, and with aching head.

"He will make some objection to tying a nuptial knot when the woman in the partnership is obviously far too ill to answer to her responses. This, unfortunately, may cause his slight consternation, and questions could be asked. On his way back home, however, a particularly unfortunate accident will happen to him. He will not be able to tell what he has witnessed. Have I made myself quite clear?"

"You plan to murder him?" I whispered, horrified.

"Naturally. However, this will be quite unnecessary if you agree to marry me without protest. The outcome is up to you, and you alone," he continued smoothly. "If you wish to live out the remainder of your life with a dead man on your conscience, then that's your own affair."

"You couldn't kill him!" I protested. "They would hang you."

He started to laugh.

"Hang me? Oh, my dear, how little you know about me! Why, in my village, it is *I* who give judgement on others. I have sent many men to the gibbet for their misdeeds, and I hardly think an 'accident' to the clergyman would be attributed to me. There are ways and means, my dear," he finished in a lazy drawl. "Now, will you take another glass of this very special ratafia?"

I managed to turn over in the bed and bury my face in the pillow. I was in the depths of despair. I could turn neither way without harming myself. But to be a party to the murder of an innocent man? Never!

"Very well, Sir Edward," I replied, my voice muffled. "I will do exactly as you wish."

I heard his sigh of relief, then the scraping of the chair when he stood up. I knew he was looking down at me, but refused to turn and face him.

"I shall always be grateful to you, Elaine," he said, in a strange voice.

Then he hurried from the room.

I lay back against the pillows, gazing at the canopy above my head. I had tried, but to no avail. Destiny had decreed that I was to become Lady Elaine Reynauld, wife to Sir Edward, Tyrant.

* * *

The wide gold ring on my finger felt strangely heavy, and I could not help looking at it. The marriage service had been performed in that bedchamber where I had been carried some hours beforehand. The innkeeper's wife and Parker acted as witnesses. Before the rector began the ceremony, he came over to me and asked whether this marriage had been entered into without undue duress. I wondered what might have transpired between himself and Parker, to prompt such questioning, but my voice was perfectly clear and calm when I replied.

"Yes. I wish with all my heart to marry this man."

How could I shout out: No! No! I am doing it solely to save you! I will not be a party to cold-blooded murder.

The carriage rattled and jolted over a badly rutted lane, and I had to cling to the strap to prevent myself from falling towards my new husband. Now that his mission had been accomplished, he appeared to have lost interest in me, for which I was especially thankful.

We were crossing a lonely stretch of open heathland where the wind blew hard. The carriage rocked and our pace slowed. I looked out of the window and caught a glimpse of the sea. My hand flew to my throat, for this was the first time I had ever seen it. I craned my neck, twisting my head from side to side, in order to see past the scrubby trees which grew at intervals along the side of the road. I had expected to see a vast expanse of blue water, but this was a thin line of grey.

"It will increase as we get closer home," Sir Edward's voice startled me, "You will find it very beautiful, yet it has its evil moments."

I said nothing.

The trees were a strange shape; looking as if a pair of giant clippers had cut the branches in one direction, forming an upswept pattern. I could not help my eager question:

"Why are the trees like that?"

"Because of the prevailing wind. They have grown with those smooth, trimmed shapes by the action of the sea winds that normally blow in the same direction throughout the entire year. Down there, near the water lies my home and the village."

The horses seemed tired. Our pace had slowed considerably. I knew that they were head down into the wind. Suddenly Sir Edward tapped on the roof with his cane and the carriage stopped. He leaned out of the window and called up to Parker:

"Halt at the crossroads."

"Yes, Sir."

The vehicle moved on about fifty yards and then stopped completely.

"Elaine, come here!" my new husband commanded. I turned my head and then gasped as I saw the object to which he was now pointing. It was silhouetted in the window: heels dangling, clothes ripped by the winds and rain, and a heavy chain clanking from the feet.

"Look!" Sir Edward commanded angrily. "The gibbet!"

I had averted my eyes after my first glimpse but now I raised them, nausea in my throat.

"What . . . what did he do?" I managed to gasp.

"He disobeyed my orders."

"Is that all?" I asked boldly, and was rewarded by a flash of anger from those dark eyes.

"It was quite sufficient. He had disobeyed me once too often."

"But you can't hang a man for nothing!" I protested.

"In my village, my word is law. As, no doubt, you will swiftly learn. The theft of a piece of bread warrants an equal punishment. Your life has been too sheltered in that orphanage, my dear. Yet you will soon learn." He rapped on the roof with his cane and the vehicle started to move off again. My eyes followed that awful, sad figure as it twisted and clanked in the wind. I saw with horror that its eyes had been stolen by carrion birds.

I now understood why Parker had been

so loath to help me, and I was thankful that I had not been so unwise as to betray him by a reproving look or word.

And so we came at last to Reynauld Hall. In spite of my predicament I could not help a tiny thrill of excitement when I saw its grandeur. It was larger than I had expected, with its Elizabethan gables and twisted chimneys. Ivy and creeper covered its graceful walls and mullioned windows stared back at me like so many unseeing eyes. Behind it rose a large, rounded hill which afforded protection from the Atlantic gales that roared in from the sea during the winter months.

We approached the house over a small bridge which forded a marshy stretch of land.

"Where is the village?" I asked eagerly, for I had seen no signs of other habitations.

"Over there," my husband replied with a sweep of his arm. "At the water's edge."

I followed his eyes and was just able to make out a few tiny dwellings huddled together near a wide expanse of yellow sand. Then I saw the squat little tower of a tiny church a little above and to the north of the cottages.

"This is my village," Sir Edward was saying. "Miserable that it is, and full of good-for-nothings. This, my dear, is your new home. May I bid you welcome?"

The carriage rattled over the granite bridge, its wheels clattering loudly. I shuddered, but could find no cause other than a sense of deep foreboding of tragedy to come.

6

WE passed through the massive entrance into a high-ceilinged hall where all the household servants had gathered to meet us. They were assembled in order of station, headed by a comfortable-looking woman dressed in dark grey, who was introduced to me as Mrs. Jane, the house-keeper. I wished her a good day, and then passed to the cook, and so on down the line. Before I had reached halfway, I was feeling acutely embarrassed; there was no mistaking the deep pity in the eyes of these people. It seemed to me that they knew all about it, and were sorry I had been involved with their master. I knew Parker had not had the time to regale them with the details prior to my arrival, because he was still outside seeing to the horses and the carriage.

My face red, I nodded briefly to the last girl in the line: a twelve year old scullion whose chubby cheeks were covered in pimples. As I turned, I was conscious of the thought that I was not alone in this enormous place. They did not resent my intrusion.

"Mrs. Jane will show you to your rooms," Sir Edward was saying as he handed his cloak to a waiting footman.

"Thank you."

"Will you come this way, my lady?" The title sounded strange to my ears and I was not at all certain that I liked it. I followed the broad grey back up the long flight of stairs, feeling the richness of the carpet-pile sink beneath my feet. At the head of the staircase stood the bust of a man, supported by a marble column. I paused to look at it.

"Dante, my lady," Mrs. Jane told me, smiling gently. I knew she must have read my thoughts, because I was wondering whether it was the bust of one of Sir Edward's forbears. "You will find the family portraits in the gallery, my lady."

Mrs. Jane led me along a narrow passage and then halted outside an ornately carved door.

"Your rooms, my lady."

She opened the door and stepped aside to allow me to precede her into an elegantly furnished room. Here again there was a luxurious carpet on the floor, surrounded by highly polished boards. Thick velvet drapes hung at the windows, and around the massive four-poster bed. I turned my eyes away from that enormous piece of furniture: I did not want to think of its implications until they were forced upon me by my husband.

"I will send Lily to you with your luggage," Mrs. Jane was saying as she went over to a door set in the far wall. "This leads to the Master's dressing-room, and the bedchamber beyond it."

My face reddened and I was grateful for her turned back. I walked across to the long covered stool which was set at the foot of the bed, and felt its plushness with my hand.

"Are all the rooms as fine as this one?" I asked.

"Yes, my lady. The Master is very particular about such things. We are kept busy with polishing and dusting." Did I detect a sniff of disdain in her tone? I could not help wondering whether the servants' quarters were furnished in a similar fashion.

"If there's anything else, my lady?"

"I don't think so, thank you, Mrs. Jane," I replied, a slight tremor in my voice. I was totally unused to giving orders to servants and I was still very unsure of myself.

"I'll send Lily to you, my lady."

The door closed behind the housekeeper and I was left alone. My first reaction was to run towards that communicating door and search it for a lock or bolt, but its surface was bare of all accessories except a handle. I sighed. There would be no keeping out my husband, I thought.

I took a handful of dark blue velvet curtain in my hand and drew it back, to look out at the garden. I was unable to see the sea from here, because my window faced inland, away from the fierce winds. The garden was beautifully kept and the gravel of the drive even now was being swept industriously by a small boy. We had disturbed its neatness with the hooves and wheels. Plainly, my husband was a meticulous person.

I felt a slight draught and turned to see who had come into the room but no one was there. I blinked, for I was certain I was not alone. I crossed the floor quickly and tried the door handle but the door was tightly fastened. Somehow, and I cannot explain why, I had the feeling that I was being watched very closely.

I went to the ornate mirror which hung over the fireplace and traced its gold cherubs with my finger-tips. I was just being foolish, I told myself; the effects of that horrible drug had not yet passed off. My imagination was overwrought. I stared at myself in the mirror, looking over my right shoulder to the end of the bed behind me. I narrowed my eyes unbelievingly. Then I spun round to speak to the girl who was sitting on the stool.

"Are you Lily?" I asked.

There was no one in the room with me.

I ran a shaking hand over my perspiring forehead and walked quickly to the side of the bed, and sank on to it. I heard the door handle depress and looked up, hoping it would be the maid, Lily.

Instead, the door opened and my husband came into the room.

"Is everything to your liking?" he asked brusquely.

"Thank you. I am a little tired and should like to rest."

"An excellent plan, Elaine. The journey must have been a tiring experience for you."

Experience! I mocked inwardly, thinking what a ludicrous understatement he had made.

"I will arrange for your dinner to be served here."

"Thank you."

He glanced towards the inter-communicating door.

"There is no lock on it," he pointed out, in a voice of dangerous calm. "You need not hope to keep me out. I intend to fulfil my rights as your husband."

I took a deep breath and stared him straight in the eyes, before replying in an icy tone:

"Of that I am fully aware."

"However, I shall not come to you yet awhile. You bristle with hostility towards me, and no love-child can be conceived under such circumstances."

Love-child? Surely I had heard those words only recently?

"I will leave you now, my dear." He lifted my right hand to his lips and kissed it. I shuddered and he flung my hand from him with a harsh laugh. "I shall enjoy my conquest of your resistance. Unlike my other two wives, I did well to choose you. We need new blood in the family; in order to rid it of the taint and stigma of the curse."

"Curse?" I urged loudly, determined to learn more. "I hear so much about this curse and the mark left on your face by a gipsy! Why will you not tell me about it?" He was fingering the red crescent.

"I do not believe legends!" he snapped. "Memories and tales grow up from unhappinesses in the past. There is no need for it to continue into the present."

"Then why did your mark frighten those gipsies?" I wanted to know. "They would have helped me . . . until you arrived and they saw your face."

"No man can help the face God gives him!"

"But what did you do to the gipsies to make them so afraid?" I was very bold now.

"I?" he laughed. "I did nothing! My family is at fault. They have existed on legends and tales of woe throughout the generations. It is their fault that I am despised and feared. Stupid superstition!"

Yet you believe in it most fearfully, I said to myself.

He caught hold of the bed hangings and jerked them angrily.

"I want nothing but a male child! I have suffered misfortune in the choice of my first two wives. I do not speak of them now, because both failed me in their proper duty towards the family. But you are different! You come from strong stock and are a stranger to this part of the country. My mistake was to marry into families of those who have lived as neighbours for many long years. The Reynaulds need new, fresh blood. Yes, we shall have a child!"

I had heard of men desirous of begetting an heir to their name, but this fanatical attitude of Sir Edward's seemed to be far beyond the bounds of normality.

To go to such lengths to procure a mother for a child . . . who had yet to be born . . . I could not help wondering whether there might be madness in the Reynauld family. I looked up into Sir Edward's face. He was stroking his birthmark as he mused:

"We will beat this together." Then he spun round and hurried from the room.

Immediately he had gone, Lily came into the room, carrying my small bag.

"Is this all you had, my lady?" she asked incredulously.

"At the moment, yes."

"Then 'tis true what Parker just said?"

"What was that?" I asked, completely forgetting myself; I was still too new a bride to remember the old adage about not listening to servants' gossip. Wide-eyed, Lily came over to me, wringing her hands.

"Like he said, Miss. You didn't know you was coming here."

"Lily! That will do!" I tried to sound firm but failed miserably. She flung herself down on the floor beside me and clutched my legs.

"Oh, Miss, go away!" she begged. "Go

away while you can! You shouldn't have come. 'Tis an evil house!"

"Get up, Lily!" I scolded wearily. "You're just being fanciful." I noticed the direction of her eyes and looked down to where my right fingers were twisting the gold band on my other hand. I flushed.

"I'll be doing the unpacking, my lady," Lily said and started to bustle around the room. There was very little for her to do, although she made a great deal out of nothing; in order to give us both time to hide our mutual embarrassment. Suddenly I asked:

"Are you a local girl, Lily?"

"Yes, Miss. I mean, your ladyship. My sister's in service five miles from here and I wanted to go too, only the Master wouldn't let me." I saw her scowl. "There was a place for me, as well, but he said I wasn't to leave."

"Why not? Surely the hiring of staff is Mrs. Jane's province, not Sir Edward's?"

"Yes, Miss, but my brother works in Sir Edward's tin mine over along, and he said that if I left, Jamie would have to go too. And Jamie didn't want to go."

"Surely he could have found another job?" I asked, intrigued by this family saga.

"Yes, Miss, but not one with a cottage as well. I mean, your ladyship, I know 'tisn't much of a place, but 'tis home for Jamie and Elsie and their two babbies."

"If you wanted to be with your sister, surely Mrs. Jane might have found a position for her in this house?" I asked, remembering the vastness of the rooms I had seen so far, and the obvious opulence of their furnishings. Plainly my husband did not suffer from lack of money.

"No, my lady, Sir Edward didn't want Rosie here because she's sweet on one of the lads in the stables. He says 'twould take Rosie's mind off her work if she were near Albert. Not that I see it," she finished, with a pout. "Rosie's me twin sister, too, Miss, and she and I like to be together. But Jamie come afore her or me, so here I be and there she be, till Albert gets a better job and they can be married."

"In that case, why doesn't your sister marry Albert now and live here with

108

him?" I asked, making a neat sum from untidy ends.

"Because the Master wouldn't have it, Miss. I mean, your ladyship. Won't give Albert a cottage, yet there be two or three going empty in the village. He's a hard man, Miss, and not many of us like him, but us can't just leave, cos he'd make it worse for those left behind."

"Nonsense!" I laughed.

Lily folded a worn shawl and draped it over her arm, then came to me with burning eyes.

"It bain't nonsense, Miss. He can do proper, harsh things once he's took a mind to it. And Rosie and me don't want to risk his wrath, so we does what we'm told."

"Lily, what is all this about a gipsy curse?" I asked, greatly daring. The girl shrank back, her eyes wide.

"Ooh, Miss, and you don't know! That's what you've come for, isn't it? To break the curse. Everyone knows it."

"Please tell me about it," I said forcefully. "How can I be expected to break the curse . . . if there is such a thing . . . if I don't know what it is?" I was beginning to get impatient with the girl's dithering.

"Oh, there be one right enough! My Ma told me all about it and she got it from her Ma, and her from her Ma. Been going for years and years, but you're the one who's got to break it. Everyone thought the other two Lady Reynaulds would do so, but they died without babbies."

"Why are babies so important?" I wanted to know.

"Because 'tis the seventh generation, that's why, my lady." Lily declared, as if her words would shed intense light over the gloom of my ignorance. "When the babby comes, the curse will go." Her face saddened. "But they both died and the babbies died too, afore they were born."

"Seventh generation?" I mused. "Is there some inherited illness in the family?"

"Inherited, what's that mean, Miss?"

I explained carefully but Lily shook her head.

"I don't know, Miss. We only hear what we're told. The baby will save the

110

Reynaulds . . . if they be worth saving!" she finished with a fierceness that did not surprise me as much as it might have done a few days earlier. "Can I go now, Miss? I mean, my lady? I got work to do downstairs, but you can always ring if you be wanting anything. I be coming back with your dinner later on, Mrs. Jane says."

"So I understand. Thank you for your help."

"Been a pleasure, Miss . . . I mean . . . my lady."

She bounced from the room and I could not help feeling sad at her departure. Her fresh candour had appealed to me; while, at the same time, it had also alarmed me. Apparently there were facts about the Reynaulds which were known to everyone but myself. I had to find out more! But whom could I ask? Obviously, Sir Edward would not tell me himself, and servants' gossip was rarely accurate.

I sat and thought about my position for a while and finally reached the simple conclusion that a vast mountain had been built out of a tiny molehill, helped in its construction by a disfiguring crescent mark on Sir Edward's face. Fanciful tales had been weaved around the family after the unfortunate deaths of both the first and then the second Lady Reynauld. Perhaps they had both been delicate and unable to stand the strain of child-bearing? Maybe Sir Edward was right in his surmise that new blood needed to be brought in from outside the county of Cornwall.

The more I thought about it, the more convinced I became that I had reasoned correctly. I was not superstitious like the members of a small village community. Because of the birthmark, the story of the gipsy's curse must have found extremely fertile ground in which to grow.

Of course, there was no denying that my own abduction had been audacious and cruel. In a way, I wished that Sir Edward had seen fit to discuss the matter with me. Yet how would it have sounded in the dreary orphanage sitting-room? Marry me and give me a male-child! Mrs. Crane would have suffered apoplexy at such a proposal, because there would have been no question of her allowing Sir Edward to converse with me alone.

Then why could he have not told the truth as soon as our journey had started? Would my own reactions have been any different? Was I that much of a fool to have said: of course I'll become your wife! I think I should have been shocked and horrified at anything approaching the truth and, what is more, I *still* should have made my bid for freedom.

Freedom! I pondered that word with care. I had broken away from the tight discipline and regulations of the orphanage; therefore I had found some freedom in my way of life. I had chosen to marry a stranger with my own free will . . . under duress! Which, I decided wryly, was definitely not a form of freedom after all! I had come here to live and would probably be allowed to do as I wished, on condition that I submitted to my new husband and provided him with an heir.

Surely I had found freedom of a kind?

I was too tired to consider the matter further. I knew instinctively that once the male child had arrived, I should be my own mistress and free to act the role of mother as I chose. Would it not be better for me to welcome the advances of my husband and get it over and done with? Was it so distasteful, this fusion of bodies, of which I had heard whispered so much in awe and speculative mirth?

When eventually I went to bed, I lay awake in the darkness for a long time, until the fire became but a feeble red glow. My eyes sought that communicating door, but the handle remained firmly at rest.

Then I fell asleep. I do not know for how long I slept, neither can I explain what noise awakened me. Perhaps I had not awakened at all and was still in a deep dream.

There was a little moonlight coming through the gap between the curtains where I had pulled them apart to open the window. I had a feeling that I was no longer alone, and my hands balled into fists. I arched my body, almost as if I was expecting Sir Edward to cover it at once with his own, and then turned to look at that door. The handle had not moved and the door was still tightly closed.

Yet I was not alone! I knew someone was in the room with me! I peered into the gloom, and a movement near the fireplace directed my eyes there. I was not afraid. I don't think I was ever afraid when we were together. Instead, I was conscious of an intense sensation of grief, yet it was not my own sorrow.

The figure approached the bed and I recognized it as being the woman who had been sitting on the stool earlier in the day. I wondered wildly whether there was some entrance to my room unknown to myself.

"Who are you?" I whispered into the darkness. "What are you doing here?"

The figure paused, and I saw her lift a candle-holder nearer to her face so that she could get a better view of the bed. In that strange, blue-tinged light, I saw her face so clearly! It was dark and very beautiful, with long, jet-black hair. In one ear hung a wide, glinting ear-ring.

"Please tell me who you are!" I urged and reached out a hand to touch her long dress with its strangely fashioned collar and sleeves.

A breeze ruffled the curtains and made

a sound like a soft sigh. To me it sounded like one word:

"Yasmin."

My hand fell away and I was asleep at once.

When I awoke to find the sun streaming through the window, I realized that I must have dreamed up my strange nocturnal visitor. Obviously the effect of Sir Edward's drugs would take some time to vanish completely.

7

"THE Master has gone to the mine, my lady," Mrs. Jane informed me as I paused at the foot of the staircase to enquire his whereabouts. "He always leaves early in the morning."

"When may I expect him back?" I asked, my spirits rising.

"Not until this evening, my lady. He told me to show you over the house."

Told Mrs. Jane! I thought grimly. No possible concern for any plans I might have in mind. On the other hand, it was only natural I should wish to learn the geography of this house as soon as possible, now that I was its present mistress. I pulled myself together and smiled at the housekeeper.

"Thank you, Mrs. Jane. Where would you care to start?"

"I thought the ground floor, my lady. Not all the rooms are in use, you understand, because his lordship does not entertain at all." She stepped aside deferently but I urged her to walk in front of me. Her grey skirts swished over the polished boards, and the bunch of keys dangling from her waist rattled and whispered. I wondered fleetingly whether she would be relinquishing them to my keeping, but was shy of asking.

We passed a narrow passage, whose walls were papered in a thick, leathery type of cloth which was sombre in hue, thereby making the place dark and gloomy. There were no ornaments or pictures; strategically placed candle sconces for night use were the sole wall ornaments. At the far end of this passage, Mrs. Jane unlocked a door and stood back to allow me to enter a massive room.

"This is the ballroom, my lady."

Its vast floor shone with polish and the dustcloths on the furnishings were clean. Chandeliers suspended on thick chains were also shrouded like forlorn ghosts.

"We clean in here once every three weeks, my lady," the housekeeper told me by way of explanation. I smiled at her.

"It is very well kept."

"Thank you, my lady."

The remainder of the ground floor held very little of interest until we came to a door which Mrs. Jane informed me was my husband's study.

"Mr. Polkerris will be working in there this morning, my lady."

"Mr. Polkerris? Who is he?"

"Sir Edward's bailiff and overseer to the mine. He comes here once or twice a week."

"Then we will not disturb him," I replied gaily and passed the closed door. I had no wish for Mrs. Jane to learn that I was eager to make the acquaintance of this gentleman. One day, I told myself, I might find myself desperately in need of an ally within this place . . .

We came to a long, narrow room which was instantly recognizable as the gallery. Portraits hung on every wall and I thought their heavy frames particularly depressing.

Men and women in all manners of dress stared disapprovingly from the walls, and I promised myself a second visit in order to inspect them more carefully.

Beyond the gallery were some more

rooms, all locked. Mrs. Jane opened each one and I took cursory glances into their shrouded interiors. Then we made our way up to the first floor where there seemed to be even more rooms than those on the ground floor.

"The Master told me to tell you that the dressmaker is coming from Bodmin this evening," Mrs. Jane said suddenly.

"Dressmaker?" I asked stupidly. "Why?" Then I blushed red, remembering my very meagre wardrobe. My companion's eyes were compassionate and I knew Lily could have lost no time in reporting my pauper's state to the servants' hall.

"She will be put in the green-room, as usual," Mrs. Jane was saying. "Then Annie and Sheila will come up from the village to help with the stitching. Good, hard workers, both," she told me approvingly. "Give them a straight seam to sew and you'll not go far wrong, that's what I always say. But when it comes to the twiddley bits, like button loops, then they be quite lost." The keys jangled and clanked. "This be the green-room, my lady."

We passed from one room to the next

and then missed out one locked door. I think Mrs. Jane must have been hoping I would not notice, because she blushed when I said:

"What about in here, Mrs. Jane?"

"My lady, that be closed for the time, if you please." She refused to meet my eyes.

"All the same," I went on firmly, "I should like to see inside."

The door was unlocked and I stepped into a room. I gasped with surprise at the lightness of the wallpapers and curtains, but it was the furniture that really took away my breath.

"But . . . " I protested, my eyes passing from wooden cradle to toy cat on wheels, from piled baby linen to rag doll sitting on the window sill.

"Yes, my lady," Mrs. Jane's voice was very gentle. "This be the nursery wing. Beyond the other door; the schoolroom, and then the governess's own bedchamber."

I was bewildered. It seemed to me that I had suddenly intruded into another world: one in which the child who lived here had run out to play in the fresh air. Everything was placed ready for use. Wooden building blocks had been stacked willy-nilly near the fireplace and a book lay open beside them. Without realizing what I was doing, I stepped forward, bent down and automatically picked it up and shut the pages. I turned to look at Mrs. Jane. There was no need for words between us. I think our expressions held our thoughts.

We shut the door and locked it firmly behind us. I passed a hand over my brow.

"I think that must be all for today, Mrs. Jane," I said wearily. "I can see the rooms in the other wing later."

"No one goes there now, my lady. They are all empty."

"Then there is no need for me to see them at all."

"May I bring you a drink of something hot, my lady?" I shook my head. "Perhaps a small glass of shrub?"

"What is that?"

"Sweetened fruit juice, my lady. You can have it with either hot or cold water. Cook has bottles put away till needed. She can get one out."

"No thank you, Mrs. Jane. I think I'll take a walk down to the village for about an hour."

"Very good, my lady. I'll send Lily to bring your cloak."

I made my way back to my bedchamber where I poured a little water into the china bowl and washed my face and hands. The rooms had been scrupulously clean, but I felt I needed to refresh myself. I could not tear my mind away from that nursery . . .

How desperately Sir Edward wants a child! I thought.

I was crossing the hall towards the front door when a hurrying figure almost collided with me. It came from the passage along which Mrs. Jane and I had walked some time before, and then pulled up abruptly when our paths converged.

"Good gracious!" said a man's not unpleasant voice. "Beg pardon! In a devilish hurry. May I?" He stepped in front of me and opened the door, bowing low from the waist in an attitude I knew to be distinctively mocking.

"I presume you must be Mr. Polkerris?"

I replied in an icy tone. He grinned at me, and I could not help liking the clean-cut features, deep blue eyes and the brown hair tied neatly with a black ribbon at back-of-head level.

"Robert Polkerris, at your service, my lady."

Was he mocking me? I wondered as I saw the keen gaze he flickered over my poor quality clothes. His own, too, had seen better days, and there was a large patch sewn on the elbow of his coat. For some reason, I felt saddened.

"If you will forgive me, your husband is expecting me before noon." Again that taunting bow and then he vanished as swiftly as he had arrived.

"Wait! Oh, please wait!" I called after him, but he was already out of earshot, striding across the drive with those long legs of his.

Why had I called after him? I did not know. Perhaps I wanted to ask more about him and the work he did, or was I so starved of friendly company that I would have done anything to persuade him to remain and converse with me? He might have been able to enlighten me about the curse. I could not ask the servants . . .

I walked over the bridge away from the house and then took a narrow lane leading towards the sea. It was a distance of a quarter of a mile to the village and I was looking forward to seeing it. I wondered how many people lived and worked under the egis of Sir Edward. Did he treat them well? The household servants seemed happy and cared for, I thought. They had food and a roof over their heads and, no doubt, gave good service for this. But what of the tales I had heard in the past few days?

The lane became coated with a thin carpet of yellow sand as I approached the sand dunes. I had been unable to visualize their full extent from the house, and was now quite surprised to see how the land sloped away towards the yellow beach beyond the dunes. The village itself was hidden by these dunes, but one came upon it suddenly after a bend in the lane. I paused and looked at the tiny cottages. My heart skipped a beat and I wondered if perhaps I had come to the wrong dwellings. This could not be a rich man's village!

Holes gaped in thatch, some windows were without panes, and the timber of their frames had almost rotted away. The tiny strips of land in front of these miserable looking dwellings were overgrown and wild with tangled marran grass. Smoke gusted from one chimney only.

I walked on slowly, my eyes on these poor homes. Were they derelict? I heard the low crying of a child, then a voice shouting to someone to be quiet. One door banged to and fro in the wind, and I noticed that it had no latch. A frayed piece of twine served to keep it shut . . . but this must have snapped.

I stood in the lane, my hands clasped tightly together. A face appeared at one of the windows and I saw fear and suspicion in its whiteness.

I took a few more steps and the face vanished, to reappear a moment later at the front door. A grubby, ill-clad and thin child clung to the woman's waist, whimpering.

"Get you gone, maid!" she yelled at me, shaking her fist. "Get you gone afore he does to you what he done to us!"

The door banged shut again and then teetered on its one remaining hinge. I was shaking. I did not understand what I had seen. Sir Edward lived in luxury and Reynauld Hall was a place that lacked for nothing. Even the rooms he did not use were kept in a state of readiness. I wondered how many hours of hard elbow grease had gone into the mirror-like polish on those floors in the downstairs rooms. Then I thought: when had they last been used?

I walked on and passed other cottages; some in a reasonable state of repair, others plainly almost derelict. One or two were quite empty. It annoyed me to see that of those which stood empty, three were in a better condition than the inhabited ones.

Why had Sir Edward not done something to effect repairs to his property? With all his wealth, each of these dwellings could have been re-thatched, re-rendered, and all the other sundry repairs carried out without even a tiny rent appearing in his money pocket.

I knew well what it meant to live in poverty!

If Robert Polkerris was the estate manager, why then had he done nothing to help the tenants?

I am a very determined person and I made up my mind then and there to take two courses of action; firstly, I would speak to Robert Polkerris and, secondly, to my husband. If the latter refused to do anything to ameliorate matters, then I would show him that I, too, could prove stubborn. I would flatly refuse even to make the effort to love him. If a love-child was needed to save the family line, then he, Sir Edward, would have to mend his ways considerably before such a child was conceived.

Of course, said a small voice at the back of my mind, he can come to you whenever he feels like it, and force a child on you.

But it won't be a love-child! Somewhere there was a subtle difference, and I had heard people say that those conceived in love were always of a happier disposition than those not.

A movement to my left caught my eye

and I turned to see the ugliest young man staring at me. I gasped, for his face seemed to be a twisted mass. He was standing just inside a broken-down fence belonging to one of the cottages, and there was venom in the look he gave me. I swallowed hastily and nodded.

"Good day to you," I said, forcing a cheerfulness into my words, and determined not to let him perceive my fear of him. I took a couple of steps nearer and then I knew I had no need to be afraid. His ugliness stemmed from the long scar which swept from high up on his forehead, across the left eye and down the line of his nose, finishing up below the right side of his mouth. The lips drooped as if it had lost its elasticity.

"Day to you, Ma'am," came the reply.

"I'm Lady Reynauld," I told him, going even closer.

"Aie. I know. Been told all about you. Ma says, can you come in?"

I looked past him to the open door of the cottage and then nodded.

"Of course. I'd like to very much."

The young man turned and led the way towards the cottage, and I followed until we were inside a small room. I realized this must be the only one on the ground floor, for it comprised both living-room and kitchen. A fire burned in the hearth while, before it, tightly wrapped in blankets, sat an old woman. Her face was encircled by a red shawl.

"Ma. She's come. Like you said she would." The red shawl moved and I found myself under the scrutiny of sharp, green eyes. For a moment I was reminded vividly of the tabby cat which skulked in the kitchens at the orphanage, tolerated only for his skill in rat-catching.

"Come over here, maid, and let's be seeing you."

I obeyed. I don't know why I was so willing to accede to this tiny, frail little person, but my feet brought me to her side almost before I was aware of the fact.

"This is Gabriel, my son. He makes a living for us both by selling seaweed to the farmers for manuring their ground. Bain't much of a job, but it does, doesn't it, my lover?" She turned those green eyes on her hideous son and I caught the flash of deep love between them.

"That I do, Ma. I pulls the cart myself. Bain't much I can't do now I have to." His voice ended on a bitter note and I wondered what particular tragedy had hit them.

"Perhaps my husband could find you a job?" I suggested helpfully, although how I was to achieve this I was not then certain. Gabriel laughed harshly.

"A job with Sir Edward?" He fingered his face. "And risk getting another one like this? I were lucky he didn't turn me out of this cottage, like he said, but Ma talked him out of it somehow, didn't you, Ma?" His hand folded over the woman's shoulder and I caught once again that flash of love between them.

"I'm sorry," I muttered, conscious that I had blundered badly.

"'Tis nothing, maid. You weren't to know. My Gabriel, he made a mistake one night, with Sir Edward's brood mare. She were in foal and 'twas a difficult breech birth. Mare and foal died, and Sir Edward said 'twas all Gabby's fault. Stable-hand he was in them days. Lost his temper, did my Gabby, and told Sir Edward that he didn't have no right to blame him for their deaths. Sir Edward cut him about the face with his knife. Shouldn't have done that."

"I'm so sorry!" I whispered, appalled at this revelation.

"Gabriel was turned away and, if it hadn't been for the help from someone who must be nameless, we'd have had to leave this cottage," the old woman explained. "My hands are bad now. I can't sew or spin as I used to. Bain't no help to the fisherfolk, nor no one else. But my Gabby does his best and works hard for his old Ma."

My respect for the ugly young man increased.

"I wish I could help," I replied sadly.

"We knew you'd come," Gabriel's mother continued. "Gabby saw you from the fields near the gibbet day you arrived. Lucky he weren't sent to the gibbet, they said afterwards, but he was saved . . . God bless him."

"Who?" I blurted out.

"Bain't telling," Gabriel said mysteriously. "I saw you and him last afternoon and I told Ma that another had come to give the master a baby."

"He wants a love-child," his mother explained, as if I had not yet understood my position! "But he won't get one. There bain't a spark of love or compassion in that man's soul. The line will die, as she said all those years ago. Come to the seventh generation and the Reynaulds will die out. Unless they be saved by a love-child." She smiled at her son again. "But he won't be getting no love-child like you, son!" Then she turned her gaze upon me. "My Gabriel's a love-child, sure enough."

"Aie. Bastard Gabby they call me in these parts," he affirmed with pride. "But I bain't ashamed of it. I be proud of me Dad. Drowned he were, afore he could make an honest woman of Ma."

I was bewildered at this recital of family history, and decided the time had come for me to leave.

"I . . . I ought to get back home now," I said, trying to be firm.

"Not till Ma told your fortune," Gabriel said, placing himself between me and the door. "That's what you be here for . . . to have your fortune told."

"Am . . . am I?" I echoed.

"Of course. All the little maids come here to Ma. She got the second sight, you see. Other two ladies come, but t'weren't no good for them, were it, Ma?"

"Come, my dear, let me have your hand."

I hesitated, and then found my arm taken in Gabriel's gigantic palm and led close to his mother's chair.

"Put the stool for her, son."

The stool was brought and I sat down while the old woman turned my hand this way and that, to catch the light from the fire.

"Aie. You be the one," she said at last, her piercing eyes searching my face. "You be the one he be looking for, and the evil will be lifted. She'll come to you soon, I reckon. But don't be afraid of the shades, little maid. They can't harm you. You are protected by an aura."

"An aura?" I asked, completely out of my depth.

"Aic. The gipsy gave you a charm. Wear it!"

I was startled, for until that moment, I had forgotten the tiny charm dropped into my hand by the gipsy man. I fumbled in the folds of my skirt and drew it out. The old woman took it from me, looked at it, and then returned it.

"Keep it with you . . . always . . . and you'll see her. She'll show you what to do." She sank back against the chair and closed her eyes. "My hand aches from holding yours. Go now, little maid, and be not afeared. There's a great love waiting for you after this is over."

I watched the old woman's face until Gabriel's hand on my shoulder bade me rise. I did so. He took me to the door and then said:

"Ma know what's she saying. Take heed."

"Has she ever told your fortune?" I asked suddenly. He smiled, the scar twisting like a country lane, and the droop of his lips more pronounced than before.

"Me? No. Wouldn't be right to tell your own flesh and blood. Lose all her power, and the maids from the village seek her advice at times . . . for a halfpenny, if they can afford it."

"Thank you for inviting me in,

Gabriel," I said, holding out my hand. He looked sheepish and then thrust his paw forward.

"You be a good one right enough," he said, and then darted back into the cottage, leaving me to walk away from the village, my mind in a whirl.

8

MY feet brought me back to Reynauld Hall but my mind was far away. So much had happened to me in less than a week that I was not sure how much had been dreamed and how much reality. The touch of those gnarled, arthritic hands had been real enough, but what of her words? Why did everyone talk so strangely? I knew I should have to discover the truth for myself, but whom could I ask? Lily, perhaps? No. I must not gossip with the servants. Besides, she was very young. Mrs. Jane? Her fifty or so years would have behind them the wisdom of experience. My husband? Not he. My questions had been rebuffed already, and I knew he would tell me nothing.

What had happened in this household to cause fear and hatred. My first glance of Gabriel had shown venom, but he did not know me! Why should he hate me initially? Or was it hatred of the name I bore? When I had been inside his house, talking to his old mother, the expression had been absent from his eyes.

I put my hand to my head, for it felt as if it were reeling. How much of this was due to an overwrought imagination, I did not know. I have had very little experience of the effects of drugs; perhaps the drinks I had been given had a lasting potency?

I reached the house and went inside. It was quiet within the hall, and I took the stone staircase slowly. At the top I paused. I do not know what drew my eyes towards the passage leading away from my own rooms, but I found myself looking intently along it. A woman was walking away from me. I thought that the dressmaker from Bodmin had arrived sooner than had been expected, and decided to make myself known to her, I quickened my pace and went after her.

I saw her pause outside a small door at the far end of the passage, and then go into the room. I could not call after her because, stupidly, I had not enquired of her name from Mrs. Jane. I reached the door and went into the room after her.

It was quite empty and totally devoid of furniture.

I was startled. Then I realized that Mrs. Jane had told me earlier that the green-room was in the same wing of the house as my own rooms.

Four, blank walls stared back at me. The windows were tightly closed and the bare floorboards looked cold and uninviting. The woman was nowhere to be seen.

"Is anyone here?" I asked, my voice echoing in the emptiness. "Where have you gone?"

A branch from a tree outside tapped on the window, making me jump. Now you're getting fanciful! I scolded myself angrily. You have been seeing things again! I crossed to the window and looked out on to the marsh. I was the only person in a vast expanse of loneliness. The skin began to crawl on the back of my neck, icy cold, and I knew I was no longer alone.

I turned round very, very slowly, and saw the woman quite clearly. She was facing me, yet she was not looking at me. Her hands were clasped in anguish, and some of her pain came through to me with such physical force that I wanted to cry out. Her attention appeared to be riveted to something that lay on the floor between us. I looked down, but there was nothing there.

I suppose I ought to have been terrified, but I felt no fear. I think I knew even then that my strange visitor was not of this world. Something greater than myself brought my hands from my side and extended my arms towards this woman. I said aloud:

"Tell me how I can help you."

Then she looked up and I was dazzled by the beauty of her sorrowing face. Tears coursed down her cheeks.

"Who are you?" I whispered. "Please tell me who you are!"

I suppose some people will say I was day-dreaming and that this woman was but a figment of my overworked brain, but to me she was very real.

I took a step towards her and saw her dress move slightly as she backed away from me.

"Oh, please don't go!" I cried.

Then I was alone again.

I could not help staring down at the floor, as if to see what had drawn her attention. The boards were darker here, and it was difficult to see the reason for this; so I sank down on my knees. My fingers traced the irregular outline of the strange mark and the notion struck me with terrifying suddenness. This was no other than an old blood-stain!

The door swayed on its hinges and squeaked mournfully. Then a draught howled along the passage, flowing cold about my crouching body. Unmistakably, I caught once more that whispered moan:

"Yas-min."

I stood up. My mind was resolute. I left that room. I shut the door and I ran back towards the staircase and my own rooms, where I rushed to the bell-pull and tugged it madly. It seemed ages before Lily came to my bidding.

"My lady?"

"Fetch Mrs. Jane to me at once!" I ordered.

"Yes, my lady. At once, my lady!" The girl's eyes were scared.

I paced the floor impatiently and then

flung away my shawl across the bed. There came a knock at the door and Mrs. Jane bustled into the room, her skirts crackling as they swept over the carpet.

"Is something wrong, my lady?" she asked, warily.

"Yes, Mrs. Jane. Please sit down." I indicated the stool at the foot of the bed. "Tell me, Mrs. Jane, who is the woman who walks this house?"

I saw the pallor of her cheeks, the frightened expression reach her eyes and the sudden shudder of her ample bosom as she gasped:

"Then you've seen her already?"

"Seen *whom*, Mrs. Jane?" I was feverish in my impatience. "I have been here less than twenty-four hours, and already there is a great deal I do not understand. I'd like you to explain."

"The . . . the woman you say you seen, was she young?" I nodded. "Then 'tis likely you seen the shade of Lady Yasmin." I saw her cross herself furtively. "My lady, where have you seen her?"

I told her about the room and again she gasped.

"You actually went into that dreadful room?" she echoed. "We never go there, my lady. It bain't safe to go in there."

"What do you mean? I found nothing unusual about the empty room, other than my uninvited companion."

"The maids won't go near that room, my lady. Neither will I! The Master don't go there neither."

"Then who cleans it?"

"No one, my lady."

"For how long has this been going on?" I wanted to know.

"Many years, my lady."

"But the floor is relatively dust-free!"

"Aie, my lady. The Lady Julia, she cleaned it once. Wanted to use it, but soon changed her mind. Said it scared her. Too cold in there."

I decided to change the trend of the conversation.

"Who, then, was Lady Yasmin?"

"The Master not told you?" I shook my head. "'Tis because of her that the family is cursed. They say she killed herself and her unborn child, and that the family must die out after the seventh generation." She crossed herself again and I felt impatience at the superstitious nature of Cornish folk.

"I understand the curse was of Romany origin?" I said.

"Aie, my lady. That it is, Lady Yasmin came of gipsy stock."

"I see." I mused thoughtfully, looking at the housekeeper. "Do you know anything of her story?"

"No, my lady. 'Twas so long ago, and there been so many tales of what happened that 'tis all garbled now. Her husband ill-treated her and she vowed vengeance for all time until the seventh generation, so they say."

"Who else in this house has seen her?"

"No one, my lady." She stared into my eyes with a mingled expression of grief and wariness. "They say that she shows herself only to those about to die."

"I see," I replied slowly. "Then you think I shall soon leave this world?"

"Could be, my lady," came the uncomfortable admission.

"And my forerunners . . . Lady Julia and Lady Janet . . . did they see Lady Yasmin's ghost?"

"I don't think so, my lady. But they were afraid of her all right! I mind when Lady Julia came to this house as a bride. She was afraid of Sir Edward and afraid of the tales she been told, but her father made her marry the Master. 'Twas all arranged from their cradles, you see. Then she was expecting after six months of living here." She shook her head sadly. "You never seen such a change in a little maid! Her colour faded, great pits beneath her eyes, and an appetite less than a sparrow's. She miscarried in the third month. The Master brought down doctors from Plymouth, but to no avail. She'd lost the will to live. The Master went almost mad with anxiety . . . not on account of her, you understand, but because of the babe. He blamed her for losing it." She was wringing her hands. "In this room it was, my lady. Carrying on something dreadful, they were, with her weeping and he ranting."

"It was not Lady Julia's fault she miscarried," I commented in a quiet voice. "Such misfortunes happen to every woman; it is the normal run of things. Besides, it is Nature's way of ridding the body of a poor product. You don't expect her to produce a weakling, do you?"

"I never looked at it that way, my lady."

"It is but common sense. Survival of the fittest, I'm afraid. A cruel creed, but Nature's own. I fail to understand Sir Edward's anger at his wife, because there would have been plenty of time to bear another, healthier child."

"No, my lady. She seemed to have lost the will to live. Had a bad bleeding, and the leeches from Plymouth only made it worse, to my way of thinking, what with their letting of blood and cupping the poor little maid! And her not strong enough to blow a feather!" I admired her for her indignation.

"She got quite demented towards the end, poor maid. Kept crying out to Lady Yasmin to let her be and die in peace."

"Then you think she saw her" I asked excitedly.

"Who can say? She was that feverish she could have seen anything."

"What of Lady Janet?"

"I don't think she ever saw her, although she refused to go in the other

146

wing of the house. She went there once by herself and ran out screaming, as if all the devils in Hell were after her. Which they was, if you take my meaning, my lady."

"I have been in that room, Mrs. Jane, and there has been nothing to frighten me. Just a great sadness."

The housekeeper looked admiringly at me.

"Then you probably be the one, my lady. She's taken to you, I reckon. Taken to you because you come to set her free of her hauntings. No one else can go in that room without feeling cold and afeared."

"Tell me more about Lady Janet," I prompted, feeling that we were getting away from the main point of this interrogation.

"No love match, that. Her father needed money and Sir Edward bought Miss Janet."

History being repeated? I asked myself cynically.

"She was a big, strong maid, and fit for child-bearing. The Master brought her here and soon we knew she was expecting. He was good to her, and we were surprised, because we didn't think he had it in him. He treated her like she was the babe herself. He arranged for the nursery to be prepared; he bought toys and clothes. Time was getting on, you see, and the babby near due. Then came the birth and the doctors delivered her of a still-born son."

"Sir Edward must have been distraught," I commented quietly.

"Aie, my lady. He went down to the stables and whipped her pet dog until it died of its injuries."

I was appalled. Clammy hands clawed at my heart.

"But why? What had a dog to do with a still-born child?"

"No reason. He was just mad with grief. Better the dog than take out his rage on another human being. The lads seen him coming and ran to hide. They knew well what to expect after what he done to Gabriel Post and others like him."

"I met Mrs. Post and her son this afternoon, in the village."

"A good boy, Gabriel, but revengeful for the wrong the Master done him. Four years ago 'twas, and he's not done nothing yet, so I doubt if he will now. Better that way, to my mind, because the Master's the devil himself when he's crossed. Young Gabby got to think of his Ma. If anything happened to him, and the Master got the better of him, then she'd have nowhere to go and no money to live by."

"Then you think Gabriel might be plotting some kind of revenge for the wrong done him?"

"Not now, my lady. Time's a good healer. Things pass. But if he should be crossed again . . . " she left the rest of the sentence in the air. "But I was telling you about Lady Janet. She got fit again, then she ran away from here. Master went after her, of course. Fierce and raging he was, but he didn't find her. None of us found her until the spring . . . a few weeks ago, my lady. She ran away when the night was bad. Raining like sheets, as it do sometimes in Cornwall in the winter. She must have slipped and hurt herself, because she fell into a stream. Her body was washed down towards the sea some weeks later. Seems it must have been caught up in some weeds awhile. She left a letter which the Master burned. It must have said something about Lady Yasmin, because he was muttering something to himself by the fire when I went in to him that evening with a drink of metheglin.

"'Yasmin! Yasmin! Always Yasmin' he was saying to the flames." She looked at me speculatively. "And now you've come, like we known you would. We always said it wouldn't be long afore the Master went a-looking for another little maid to bear his babbies." Her hand sought mine in a gesture of bold familiarity. I was not displeased. Her concern touched me deeply.

"Take care of yourself, my lady. Things'll be different with you, to my way of thinking. You seen Lady Yasmin and you bain't afeared."

"No, Mrs. Jane," I replied in a clear voice. "I have seen Yasmin more than once, and there is nothing to be scared of, I am certain. I think she wants to tell me something, but I can't make out what it is. I shall go to that room again and wait for her."

"Ooh, my lady, is that wise?" Mrs. Jane shook her head. "Perhaps she be having you on, and will strike later. Friendly to start with and then an enemy afore you knows where you be."

I smiled at her.

"I disagree. I believe most strongly that she needs my help. I intend to do everything within my power to give her rest. After all, it must be very lonely walking the rooms of this house year after year. Perhaps she is tired and wishes to lie at rest for ever? Maybe it is her wish for me to bear Sir Edward's child. What have I to lose, Mrs. Jane?" I felt light-headed with the prospect of my self-imposed crusade.

"Take care, my lady! I beg you to take care!" was all my companion would say.

When she had left me alone, I sat on the side of the great bed, willing Yasmin to come to me. However, I was disappointed. Plainly she would not appear just because I gave the command.

She may have been angry with me for my attempts to summon her, I do not know, but I did not see her again for some time.

The days passed and I familarized myself with the house and the village. I saw little of my new husband and he did not come to my bed. I went on two occasions to that empty room and waited for Yasmin to join me, but still nothing happened. I knew she could not be watching me from behind, because my extraordinary sense of perception would have informed me of her ghostly presence.

She had given me her message and that was all. Perhaps I should never see her again, I thought, as I wandered disconsolately away from the empty room. Perhaps I had dreamed it all? Had I caught the superstitious mood of those who surrounded me?

As time passed, I became bored. I had worked many long hours each day as a teacher and the abrupt change from that life to this had begun to tell on me. I wondered what I could find to while away the time. Over dinner one evening

I asked Sir Edward if there was anything I could do to help in the running of the estate.

"You." he echoed with a laugh. "I have Polkerris to do all that is necessary."

"But could I not teach the children of the village?"

"The poor are illiterate and should remain so," came the cold reply. I asked, greatly daring:

"Then could I not perhaps help their mothers to care for them? On the occasions I have been to the village I've noticed how ill-kempt they are. Surely I might help?"

His dark eyes pierced mine.

"You will keep away from the village and my tenants!" he ordered. "I will not have you risking your health by mixing with them."

I lowered my eyes but my brain was active. I knew what I was going to do. I have never liked being told *what* I must do! Only fear of being turned out into the cold, unfriendly streets, had stilled my tongue from making retorts to Mrs. Crane and from biting back my own opinions. Now, however, I was my own mistress. I cared little for my husband's orders. The people in the village needed help and I was determined to give it, no matter how angry I might make him.

9

I DECIDED that there was one sure way in which I could be of use to the villagers, and that I should require the cooperation of Mrs. Jane and the cook. I asked Lily to send the former to my room.

"Mrs. Jane, I'd like to enlist your help," I told her as she stood in front of me, her hands demurely clasped.

"Yes, my lady?"

"I want you to give me a detailed inventory of the contents of the pantry." Her face registered her dismay.

"But you saw everything when I took you over the kitchens shortly after your arrival here, my lady," she protested, and then bit her lip. "Forgive me, my lady, I should not have spoken in that manner."

"It is quite all right, Mrs. Jane. I have no wish to pry or to supervise you in any way. I leave all the household arrangements in your expert hands!"

I saw her pleased expression and the relaxation of her stiffened body. "I have a plan and I need your help very badly. Won't you sit down?"

She took the proffered chair and I stood looking down at her. It was a bright spring day and the sun shone through my window on to her face.

"This has to be something of a secret between us, Mrs. Jane."

"Indeed, my lady?"

"Yes. For reasons which I will not divulge, I think we should act quietly and without fuss. Tell me, does the Master leave the purchase of food stuffs entirely in your hands?"

"Yes, my lady, but I have to give a very detailed account of them all to Mr. Polkerris, which he checks and then hands on to the Master."

"We are well stocked, are we not?"

"Oh yes, my lady. The autumn saltings were done back along; the preserves and picklings also. We have ample supplies of medicants and potions in the still-room. That were Lady Janet's doings, my lady, just before she was too heavy with child to work long hours. Then there are all the beverages. We had more than enough to outlast a long, hard winter."

"As I expected. Tell me," and I knew my eyes were sparkling, "does my husband need a tally of every mouthful we eat?" I knew him to be something of a gourmet, because he was very appreciative of good meals.

"Oh no, my lady. That would be impossible."

"Good. I'm glad to hear it."

Her comment after I had unfolded my plan was this, and it was said with a sheepish tone:

"Cook and I sometimes give the maids and stable-hands a few small titbits to take home with them on their monthly days off, but the Master doesn't know about it. We've had to be very, very careful, my lady, seeing as how he is about such things."

"I understand, Mrs. Jane. In this new venture, the entire responsibility will be mine, is that clear? I shall take the food and whatever else we can spare, so that if there should be any repercussions, they will fall on my head alone." I smiled. "I doubt if there's much he could do to punish me. Oh, and one other thing, Mrs. Jane, no word of this is to reach Mr. Polkerris's ears, is that understood?"

"But, my lady . . . " Mrs. Jane began and then shut her mouth firmly. "It is nothing, my lady. I will tell cook and she will have the first basket ready within the hour."

I knew I should be quite safe, because Sir Edward usually spent most of the day at his mine. I had heard that his discipline over there was harsh, and the wage at the end of the day very meagre. I need have no fear of interference from him. However, I did need to be wary of Robert Polkerris, as I had discovered shortly after my arrival. I had gone to the picture gallery to study the portraits of my husband's ancestors, hoping to find one of Yasmin, but she had been conspicuous by her absence. I was walking slowly down the length of the room, scrutinizing the faces, when I heard his voice behind me:

"A fearsome-looking bunch, don't you agree, Lady Reynauld?" He laughed and I spun round.

"I find them very interesting," I

retorted, a little unsure of myself. He joined me and then pointed.

"The Stuart Reynaulds . . . and here, the bewigged ancestor in the court of King James . . . his wife beside him . . . are you looking for anyone in particular, my lady?" His eyes mocked me and I felt acutely uncomfortable.

My gaze swept over those stony faces but of the darkhaired, full-lipped gipsy face there was no sign.

Robert Polkerris was still staring at me, one eyebrow raised.

"You won't find the cause of your present misery here, I'm afraid, Lady Reynauld," he teased. "She was banned to obscurity more than a century ago, that much I can tell you. It seems she brought disgrace on the family name and the then present lord of the manor could only shudder on seeing her gipsy face."

My curiosity about Yasmin had been temporarily lulled by my recent conversation with Mrs. Jane; therefore I did not rise to the bait. Instead, I said in the haughtiest tone at my command:

"Tell me, Mr. Polkerris, you are agent

and manager to my husband, are you not?"

"At your service, my lady." He made a small bow from the waist and I was unnerved by the sparkle in his eye. Was it derision, because he knew the reason for my presence in this house, or was it something deeper, more personal to himself?

"Then can you explain why I find the cottages in this village in such a deplorable state of repair? Who is at fault, yourself or my husband? If the former, then why have you not reported the matter to my husband and effected the repairs to these dwellings? I know there can be no lack of finance. One has but to look around this building to take my meaning."

His expression became guarded and his eyelids partly lowered.

"Have you brought this problem to your husband's notice, my lady?"

"Not yet, but I intend doing so with all speed."

"Then, if you would accept my advice, I should think again before speaking to him," he warned.

I immediately asked him why I should do so.

"If I may be so bold as to advise you, do not tread on to paths of which you know nothing. I have my own orders and carry them out to the letter."

I looked at him, my face registering my distaste. Then my eyes flickered over his poor clothes. I blurted out:

"Were it not for your own poor state, I should suspect you of converting the monies to your own use."

I wished afterwards that I could have bitten back my words. He recoiled from me, and his eyes were bitter.

"Thank you, my lady. If I may be pardoned for returning to my work?"

Pride kept my feet on the ground. I wanted to run after him as he turned from me. I wanted to beg his forgiveness for my cruel outburst, yet I did nothing. I had no proof! He might possibly be just as plausible a rogue as Sir Edward! For all I knew, the money could have been slipping into his own pocket and by keeping to such well-worn raiment, he could have an alibi for such theft. He looked a pauper himself!

161

It had troubled me greatly, this conversation of ours, but I had not taken steps towards an apology. I told myself again and again that he had asked for what I had said. He had openly mocked me. I was the lady of the house; respect was due to me. Just because he knew the role I was to fulfil, there had been no need to scorn me for baseness. Was I base? I do not think so. I still had much to learn, and had been brought up on tolerance, in spite of my quick temper. I had always weighed both sides of every question with care before acting upon a decision. I had walked into this marriage as a free agent . . . ignoring the threat Sir Edward had made, of course. Had I truly objected, I am sure I could have found some way out. Yet I had given in without much fight.

I vowed then and there to keep well away from Robert Polkerris. Naturally I had seen him once or twice since then, but he had not seen me. He had crossed the hall with those long strides, and I had peeped at him from the staircase above. He had not turned round . . .

I did not want to meet him whilst on my errands of mercy in the village. I did not wish to be subjected to his mockery again. Neither did I want him to report my action to my husband.

It was exciting to make plans with Mrs. Jane and cook! We robbed the still-room, swept one shelf clean in the pantry, and left three hooks empty of salted meats. Naturally I did not take all this in one visit; to transfer such goods took me all of five weeks. I even rolled up my sleeves in the kitchen and helped cook make great quantities of fuggan . . . with and without raisins . . . heavy cake, and star-gazing pasties. Cook explained to me how to make the latter. In her heavy Cornish dialect, she wagged the rolling pin at me, saying:

"Get a herring, clean 'un, and put some stuffin' as what you do have in mabiers . . . that be chicken, my lady . . . and sew'en up with niddle and cotton, putt'en in some daugh made of suet and flour; pinch daugh up in the middle and lave the heid stickin' out one end, and tail t'other. Course, to cook'en proper they should be cooked in a fringle fire crock and brandis and old furzy tobs."

By this time, I was completely lost, and began to shake with laughter. Soon we were all rolling with mirth.

"Aie!" chuckled Mrs. Jane, wiping her eyes on the corner of her big apron. "We never laughed like this with Miss Julia or Miss Janet. They were too afeared to come into the kitchen, lest cook here give notice."

"You won't do that, will you, cook?" I begged, the smile wiped from my face.

"Naw, my little lover, I do belong here and here I be stayin'."

After my first visit to the village, the inhabitants began to look for me. Usually I saw a barefooted child scuffing her toes in the sand of the dunes, and she would jump up and down, smiling and waving until I waved back, then she would be off like the wind back to her home. All the front doors were open to me, and smiles welcomed my arrival.

I grew to love these good, simple folk, and it made my heart ache unbearably to see the conditions under which they were housed. It seemed so very unfair!

I lived in an enormous house, most of which was unused, and there was warmth and comfort all about me, whilst these poor souls had to contend with gaping doors and windows, leaking thatched roofs, draughts which howled about their necks and feet, and the lack of proper nourishing food. They were stoical in their attitude, merely grinning at me and saying that it was not so bad now summer was on the way.

With the summer weather, there was no excuse for repairs to be delayed any longer, I thought.

I took old sheets, curtains and blankets from the sewing-room up at the Hall and distributed them to the villagers, telling them to cut and sew according to their needs. I helped take newly baked bread from the heat of a clome oven.

I saw Mrs. Post rub salt into a small piece of precious butter and then apply it to a whitlow on Gabriel's finger, although I protested all the while.

"No, no, Mrs. Post! You should be eating the butter, not wasting it like this!"

"'Tis Gabby's finger I be minding

most," she retorted. "How can the lad work if he be bad?"

I remained silent, but on my next visit I brought a pat of butter from the dairy and left it under a plate on the table with the shaky leg, hoping that Mrs. Post would discover it after I had returned home.

I tied roasted parings of hot turnip behind the ear of a seven year-old boy with a swollen face, and wondered how this would cure his raging toothache. The next day they brought him bellowing, to the kitchens at the Hall, begging 'my lady' to hold him whilst the tooth was extracted, because he had refused obstinately to let anyone else touch him. I thanked my good fortune that my husband was not present, otherwise there might have been some awkward explaining to do!

I like to think that I helped these people in some small way, and I know they were grateful to me. I had impressed upon them that they must not mention my name to Sir Edward, and they nodded in emphatic agreement.

"I wish I could help with repairs!" I complained on one occasion, as I was bidding farewell to Mrs. Post.

"That you can't, my lady," her son chimed in. "Better left to the other one. He does what he can."

"Sh! Gabby!" His mother's eyes were full of warning.

"May I not be told, or is it a closely guarded secret?" I asked, smiling.

"Us bain't be free to tell . . . yet," the old woman replied. "When he says we can, then we will. We promise."

With that I had to be content. It made me feel warm inside to know that someone else was trying to help these people, and I speculated as to his identity. I even tried questioning Mrs. Jane, but she saw through my subtle tactics almost at once and her mouth shut like a clam.

Naturally my husband knew nothing of my activities. He did not even ask me how I amused myself during his absence. As far as he was concerned, I had been brought to his house for one reason only. I had escaped his attentions for almost two months, but I knew this state of affairs could not last much longer. I was correct.

Before I went upstairs to bed each night, I had taken the habit of making a short walk around the gardens, to admire the flowers which were tremendous in their profusion. To look from my window across the lawns showed a vast carpet of colour, swaying gently in the light sea breeze. I walked amongst them in the evenings because it was then that their perfume was most pronounced.

It was here that Sir Edward came to me.

I was bending over a bed of sweet alyssum, when a shadow joined my own. I turned quickly, thinking it might be one of the men employed to keep the garden tidy.

"Elaine . . . stand up!" My husband's voice rang in my ears. I stood up slowly, a one-eyed daisy dangling from the fingers of my right hand.

"Sir Edward?"

"It is time we talked. Come!" He took my arm and I fell into step beside him. "Are you happier now?" he asked in a kindly tone.

"Thank you . . . yes."

"Good. And what of myself? Have you succeeded in regarding me as less than an ogre?"

I blushed. I did not want to admit that he had filled my thoughts only when my mind and hands were occupied with doing things for my villagers.

"I have kept my part of our bargain by leaving you alone these past weeks. Now, however, it is time you fulfilled yours." He paused and turned me to face him. "Our child shall be born in the New Year, when the winter winds roar about the house. February is a good month for birth; it makes a man of a boy." His hand slipped into mine and I dared not draw back. I was deeply apprehensive and afraid. He laughed, releasing me. "Go to your room and I will join you."

I remained looking at him for a moment, then I picked up the skirts of my blue dress and ran across the lawn, back into the house. The stairs were too wide for me to take two at a time, but I rushed up them, pausing for breath only when I had reached the top. I gained my room and slammed the door behind me. Lily had already laid out my cambric nightgown with its high lace collar and cuffs.

I started to undress . . .

The light faded from the world outside and I lay in the dusk, listening . . . listening . . . I heard his footsteps pass my door . . .

My eyes were riveted on that one door between our rooms. I longed for the latch to remain at rest. All too soon it lifted and the door swung open. The sheets were tucked under my chin and my fingers tightened their grip on them.

Did he know I was still a virgin? I wondered in panic. I knew I should not be able to bear it if he hurt me.

He came over to the bed and stood looking down at me. Then he smiled, and I was reminded at once of a picture of a satyr I had seen in a book at Mrs. Crane's. He sat on the edge of the bed. I did not move. His eyes did not leave mine and I found my gaze drawn by their twin, dark pools which seemed to bore into my head in the dusk. They flashed like the riding lights I had seen on ships out at sea.

170

I felt him climb in beside me and I shuddered. Then his face was touching mine and I could feel his mouth searching for my lips. I cried out in fright, then strong hands began to stroke me. I felt strange, detached, out of this world. I started to imagine that I was floating somewhere above the bed, looking down at myself and Sir Edward. Still those hands stroked and mesmerized me. His mouth was hot on mine. I felt an upsurge of feeling sweep over my body. It seemed animal-like and unnatural; rather as I had imagined the call of one beast to another. I was not myself. I felt no love or hatred. All I knew was this rush of passion, roused by skilled hands from an inexperienced body. It was quite distasteful, and I was ashamed of my response.

I opened my eyes and stared into the darkness beyond the head close to me. And I saw her quite clearly. I saw a strange light on a mocking, laughing face, where a cold ear-ring glinted in the eerie glow that came from within her. I heard her voice say inside my head:

"'It is not your child! Not yours'!"

I longed to push away her taunting face. I raised my hands to her, only to find them entwined around my husband's neck. I could not fight the tide within me. My resistance flowed steadily away. I cried out in the darkness:

"Yasmin! Yasmin!"

Her eyes seemed to grow larger and larger, until there was nothing else but these shining pools.

Then I slept.

10

ONCE again I was preoccupied with thoughts of Yasmin. Until her reappearance the previous night, I had believed her to be friendly towards me, but now I doubted. There indeed had been the fierce looks of the gipsy as she had uttered those strange words about the child not being mine. I could make no sense of them. I tried to convince myself that I had been dreaming, and that everything I had thought I had seen was nothing more than my own imagination playing tricks on me. At the time I had been undergoing a new experience; I was no longer a girl, but a woman. Was it surprising, therefore, that fancies had been born in such circumstances Had the imagined hatred been but a reflection of my own dislike of my husband and our act of love?

I wanted to shake my head to clear it, but everything I saw in the house brought back her name to me. I went from room to room, subconsciously searching for Yasmin, and I knew I had to get right away, if only for a few hours. My head rang with the words: gipsy curse!

It was a beautiful day and there was no need for a shawl over my thin dress. The heat of the sun beat on my back, warming my shoulders as I walked quickly away from the grey stone house. I had no plans; I simply allowed my feet to take me where they willed. I went towards the village, although I did not go through it; taking, instead, the lane which wound up to the squat church. It nestled between the dunes, looking almost as if it had buried itself within the sand, and hoped one day for the wind blowing in from the sea to cover it completely with its yellow grittiness. Stunted fir trees waved from side to side, and my hair slipped from its braiding to billow softly about my cheeks while I walked. Above my head trilled a lark, and I screwed up my eyes against the sun, trying to see its fluttering body. The vast blue emptiness stared down at me.

The gate creaked as I pushed it open.

I walked towards the Norman arch over the main door. I lifted the heavy iron handle and heard the metal clang of the latch. It was dark inside the church. The deeply niched windows were very small and heavily stained, so that the sun found difficulty in penetrating to the grey stone nave.

When I had become accustomed to the gloom, I explored the church, looking at the tombs and hoping, or so I believe, to find the Reynauld family vault. But there was nothing to indicate its presence inside the church itself. I went outside again and made my way slowly through the graveyard where the grass and wild flowers grew alongside each grave.

I found the thick, rusted iron railing around the family vault and clasped them with my hands, while I turned my head from side to side, trying to decipher the inscriptions on the vast granite slab beyond. A voice behind me made me jump.

"If you're hoping to find her here, you're in for a disappointment."

I spun round and came face to face with Robert Polkerris. My pulse quickened momentarily as his warm smile reached his eyes. I saw the way the breeze ruffled his brown hair, and the shadow of long lashes cast by the sun against his cheeks.

"I apologize, my lady," he continued affably. "I have startled you."

"Yes, Mr. Polkerris, you did."

He glanced again at the vault and the smile faded.

"She wasn't buried here, or so the tale goes."

"Who?" I pretended to show unconcern, but he laughed.

"Yasmin, my lady."

My hand sought the rusted railing again as I turned my face away. He came closer.

"Does she worry you very much?" he asked gently. I found myself nodding. "Shall I tell you about her?"

"Do you know the story, then?" I asked eagerly, and with interest showing keenly in my face, I am sure.

"I know more than most people. You see, my family is almost as old as yours in these parts."

"Oh!" I was startled, for I had not

realized he was a local man. I do not know why, but I had always thought of him as having been brought from out of the county to work for Sir Edward. His eyes were upon me.

"Yes. Polkerris is a family name locally. Unfortunately, we do not share the same wealth as the Reynaulds." I detected bitterness in his tone, and my gaze passed to his threadbare coat. He shrugged. "And you, my lady, are that Lily maid of Astolat."

I was startled, mainly because I had not expected him to be well versed in the works of Sir Thomas Malory. My surprise must have registered in my face, because he smiled as he continued:

"Yes, my dear Lady Elaine, I know the legends of the Cornish King Arthur. Camelot is one of our towns, you see. And you, like that Lily maid, have come to save us."

"Save you?" I echoed. "I recall nothing of such things in the tale!"

"Elaine loved Sir Lancelot, but he played her false with the Lady Guinevere; that you *do* know. Elaine gave birth to the purest and most noble of all the knights, and he succeeded in the quest for the Grail. I liken you to the Lily of Astolat. In a way, you have a quest, and will bring forth a son who is destined to break Yasmin's curse."

He was laughing at me again. I flushed to the roots of my hair at his inferences.

"Hence I said you had come to save us."

"I did not come of my own free will!" I blurted out, impassioned. His eyes narrowed and the smile vanished.

"I know. And I pity you."

"I don't need pity!" I declared and turned away from him, meaning to leave the graveyard, but his strong fingers on my wrist detained me. I glanced down at his hand and could not help noticing the sun glinting on the fine, brown hairs that curled along the back. I had a strong impulse to turn my wrist and seek his fingers with mine.

"Come!" he told me kindly. "You want to hear about Yasmin. She lies in an unknown grave. Her husband refused to allow her to rest in the family vault. She had disgraced them, or so the tale goes." He was leading me to a soft bank of grass, and soon we were sitting side by side.

He reached behind him to pull a long piece of rye grass which he then stuck between his teeth.

"They say she was very beautiful. Her husband was desperately proud of her and commissioned her portrait from one of the best painters of their time. You understand, this was shortly before the start of the Great Rebellion."

"Where is the portrait now?"

"Destroyed. After her death, Sir Geoffrey ordered everything of hers to be burned. Yet her memory lingered on. She came of gipsy stock and you can well imagine the consternation when he brought her home as a bride! The family was appalled."

I could see it all so well! The rigid disapproval of a noble family who had expected the heir to marry into a family of equal merit. Then he had brought home a girl found in a band of wandering gipsies.

"She was quite illiterate, poor girl, but Sir Geoffrey determined to change all that. Tutors came to the Hall but none remained long, Yasmin saw to that. They say that she eventually learned to read and write, but this was only because Sir Geoffrey's estate manager offered to teach her. Inevitably, this led to tragedy."

"He fell in love with her?" I prompted. Robert Polkerris smiled, as if the thought amused him.

"So it is said. This all happened during the Civil War when records have become rather blurred. The Royalists were struggling with the Roundheads for supremacy over Devon and Cornwall. It is generally assumed that Sir Geoffrey returned home one day to find Yasmin in the arms of her lover. He ran him through on the spot and, to spite him, Yasmin killed herself and their unborn child."

"Whose child was it? Her husband's or her lover's?" I asked eagerly.

"Sir Geoffrey's."

"That must explain the blood-stain I found on the floor!" I exclaimed and Robert Polkerris laughed good humouredly.

"After all these years? I hardly think so. This happened approximately one hundred and fifty years ago. Blood-stains would have faded, or have been scrubbed out long since."

"All the same," I persisted. "It is still there!"

"With each day that passes, you are becoming more like us," he teased. "You have been infected by the superstition and legends that surround you at the Hall. In a moment you'll be telling me that you have actually seen Yasmin."

"I have done so."

He did not laugh, as I had expected, neither did he comment on my statement. Instead he reached for my hands and held them tightly.

"Be careful!" he warned. "I beg you, take care!"

"You mock and tease, yet you are just as superstitious as the rest of us!" I accused triumphantly. "In a moment you'll be telling me that you believe in ghosts."

"No, my Lady Elaine, I doubt whether I'll go that far. But you mustn't forget that we Cornish folk are fey. It is inevitable because, with our vast expanse of coastline and the sea the means of livelihood to a great many, we are at greater odds with death than people who live elsewhere. Therefore we cannot be blamed for taking a light hearted and often cynical view of life . . . and a deep regard for death."

"You believe that I am in some way threatened?" I asked slowly. The grip on my hands became almost unbearably hurtful.

"Yes. By sorrow and pain. You have married a harsh, cruel man who is, I fear, sometimes on the verge of madness. Perhaps this is the curse of the Reynaulds. Who knows? A streak of insanity passing down through the ages and unconquerable by time; hence the legends that have grown up around them."

"And the crescent birthmark?"

"Just one of Nature's macabre little jokes."

I felt in my dress and withdrew the star-shaped charm I had been given. I had threaded it on to a narrow ribbon which I always tied around my waist. I handed it to Robert Polkerris without a word. He studied it thoughtfully, turning it over and over in his hands.

"Where did you get this?"

I told him.

"Then wear it always," he advised.

"Potent against the powers of evil?" I suggested laughingly but he shook his head and quoted a verse to me:

> "'From ghoulies and ghosties,
> And long leggety beasties,
> And things that go bump
>   in the night
> Good Lord, deliver us'"

"My family motto," he concluded, with a grin, and I knew he was still teasing me. "Not that it ever did much good, because we have all dispersed. I live with my widowed mother about three miles from here; my younger brother has a ship of his own, and is far away doing a bit of buccaneering . . . or so I suspect; and my sister is far too busy rearing a quiver full of youngsters on a Devonshire farm to worry about her brothers. As you see, a poor product, but honest."

"Are you?" I challenged fiercely, remembering the state of the village. "Are you perfectly honest, Robert Polkerris?"

"Yes, my lady. In all good conscience, I can say I am an honest man."

"Then why haven't you seen to the repairs that are needed?" I burst out. "You're the agent and it's your responsibility to see that all is well there."

"Yet I can do nothing if the Master decrees otherwise," his voice was sad.

"But have you *tried*?"

"Naturally."

I stood up and smoothed my dress.

"I cannot understand you! Unless you are afraid of my husband . . . "

"I have no fear of Sir Edward, but I have learned to tread with care. May I suggest you do the same, my lady?"

"What do you mean?"

"Exactly what I say. May I give you a small warning? It would go amiss if he should recognize the distinctive fabric of his own furnishings lying across the back of a certain six-year-old girl."

"Oh no!" I wailed, my hand flying to my forehead in despair. "I implicitly told her mother not to use it for clothes!"

"I fear that good woman is not

blessed with a great intelligence." He was laughing at me and a sudden fear gripped me so hard that I felt almost sick.

"You will not tell?" I implored. "You could not do so . . . "

Again that aggravating smirk. I stamped my foot pettishly.

"Oh, how I dislike you! I know your kind. You haven't the spirit or the courage to stand up to a man like Sir Edward for the villagers' rights, yet you wouldn't consider it beneath you to go crawling and bleating about the things I have done . . . and shall continue to do . . . whatever happens . . . behind his back! Go ahead, then! Tell him!"

I turned on my heels and walked quickly away, almost stumbling over the uneven ground. His infectious laughter followed me to the lych-gate. I was furious with him, and also with myself for admitting to the things I had been doing for the villagers. I tossed my head. Let him tell my husband! I thought boldly. Let him bleat and whine, I won't care! The village belongs to me just as much as it does to Sir Edward.

I did not look back as I hurried homeward. It was much hotter now, and my forehead beaded with perspiration. The house was as silent as the grave, I thought, when I paused in the hall to savour the coolness of thick stone walls. No sound but my own heavy breathing came to my ears, and I wondered where the servants were.

A movement on the staircase above caught my eye and I looked up, expecting to see either Lily as she hurried about her household tasks, or Sir Edward; although I had presumed him to be at the mine two miles away.

My hand sought the ornately carved newel post and clung to it as Yasmin came down the stairs towards me. Her face was calm but sad. Gone was the mockery of the previous night. I sensed her thoughts.

Come with me! Come with me! she seemed to be saying.

I watched her cross the hall and could have sworn that her heavily brocaded dress swished against the stone flags like the wind amongst the reeds of the marsh. Her long black hair curled down her back and I noticed a diamond clasp holding it in place. Then her left arm rose and I saw the tapering fingers as she beckoned to me.

We went into the passage and came to the door of Sir Edward's study. One moment she was there, the next I was alone. I opened the door and entered the room, knowing that I would find her within. She had stationed herself by the bookshelves to the right of the marble fireplace, and was now searching a line of leather-clad books. I stood by my husband's desk and watched intently. I saw her take out a heavily tooled volume and tuck it under her arm; then her hand disappeared into the void it had left. I saw her raise herself on tip-toe as she stretched her arm behind the remaining books, and I knew that she was groping behind them for something.

A blackbird perched on a branch of a nearby tree and burst into song with a suddenness that startled me. I blinked. When I looked again, Yasmin had left me.

I almost ran across the short distance between the desk and the bookshelf. I saw the book she had pulled out and lifted it out myself, bending down to place it on the floor in order that I should have both hands free. Then I thrust my right arm behind the remaining books and groped wildly. I touched nothing, I darted into the room to fetch a chair, and this I put close to the wall and climbed up on to it. Now I was able to touch the back of the deep bookshelf. My fingers closed over a small, thick book.

Barely able to contain my eagerness, I pulled it out and gazed at its faded and torn red leather cover. At one time it must have been beautiful, although the gold of its tooling had mostly fallen away. The pages were hard and yellow, and I had to be very careful as I opened the leaves.

The writing looked like that of a ten-year-old child, so ill-formed and untidy! The spelling left a great deal to be desired, I thought, my governess's nature asserting itself.

I prised open the flyleaf and my heart seemed to miss a beat as I read the inscription:

"Yasmin Reynauld. Her booke."

11

I DARED not remain in the study to read the book, lest my husband should return and find me there. I wondered if I should take it into the garden and settle myself on the stone seat by the ornamental fishpond, but decided this was too public a place, being overlooked by the windows on the southern side of the house. Instead, I clutched the book to my bodice and ran upstairs to my room. I pulled a chair across to the window and sat down, tucking my feet under me. Then I opened the book.

It was plain from my first glance that the writer had been under considerable stress as she put pen to paper. This came through so forcibly to me that I looked up and searched the room with my eyes, expecting to see Yasmin. But I was quite alone. She had led me to her book and seemed content to leave me to read it undisturbed.

The handwriting was laboured, and spelling mistakes increased as I read deeper into the narrative. I thought at first it was a diary, but this was not so. There were no dates at all; it was a hastily recorded chronicle of events leading up to a definite finale. I had to make allowances for some strange expressions and un-English phrases, and this is my interpretation of what Yasmin had written.

★ ★ ★

I defy my husband to destroy this! When I am gone and the memory lingers on, future generations of Reynaulds will want to know why, and how, I died. I have said this must be so.

I need not go back to the beginning; to those days in my early happiness at being the beautiful young bride of Reynauld. We were happy, then. But it was not enough for Geoffrey. He wanted to change me; to teach me. I hated them: those tutors with their long noses, black gowns and disapproval. They were afraid of me and what I could do to them. They soon left. Then Hugh Trewella began to teach me.

I think he always understood how I felt, coming to an alien world whose customs were so different from my own. He was patient and gentle and a love sprang up between us. I worked with my figures and letters, longing to please him; but this is all well-known to those I am leaving behind.

Geoffrey knew I liked Hugh and he teased me. I still loved Geoffrey and I also loved Hugh, because he understood me and was gentle.

I do not know why the war came. They both tried to explain to me but I have no knowledge of kings and Rights! I did not care. All I knew was their quarrel. I could not understand the reason for such bitterness between them, until Hugh came to say farewell. He went to join the king. Geoffrey left for Plymouth, there to stand beside the men supporting the king's enemies. I care little for who was right. All I care for is the evil he did to us later.

They did not come here. They fought within a few miles of this place yet no one came here until that day when I saw him. I was in the bedchamber and saw his poor, broken figure staggering towards the marsh and bridge which leads to the big gate. The servants brought him to me, and laid him upon my bed. He did not know me, I am sure. The wound in his head was wide and deep, and the fever great. I do not understand how he managed to reach this house! I feel that an impulse beyond himself brought him back to me.

We laid him in the far wing; in the small room whose window overlooks the dunes. I thought he would die; yet he did not do so. My herbs and potions learned from my gipsy days helped to save him. I cared little should Geoffrey return. They had been friends in the past and there was no reason why they should not be friends again. The war was over for Hugh. His mind had become like a child's. He kept calling me 'Mother'.

I cared for him, feeding him with a spoon because he could not feed himself. He clung to my skirts like a baby . . . like the baby I knew I should soon bear my husband. He was a sick child and I loved him.

That devil came home from the war, gloating over his triumphs and vowing to put all Royalists to the sword. I was foolish, I suppose, because I told him about Hugh. I took him to the room where my darling child sat playing with some clothes pegs brought from the kitchens.

I cannot bear to tell of what he did to Hugh! My only comfort is that Hugh was so child-like that he did not know what was happening to him. My husband tied him to the bedpost, the leather thongs biting into his wrists and then whipped him, demanding to be told 'Royalist secrets', as he called them. Hugh cried like a child for its mother.

The wound in his head reopened but my husband would not let me tend it. I stood, helpless, watching the blood. I thought then that Geoffrey would cease. He laughed, and his eyes glittered with a fiendish madness, and I knew he enjoyed what he was doing.

The flesh is weak and Hugh had not long recovered from the fever. His face became dulled, and eyes vacant, but still

Geoffrey tortured him.

He died where he crouched, beside the bed we had made for him in that room.

I cannot bear to think of him! It is too soon and my pain too great. I have promised myself revenge. I do not wish to live in this house. It is a place of misery and evil. I shall not bring my son into the world to be touched by my husband. He shall have no control over a son of mine!

I curse him and all those who come after. I curse the male descendants that they may live in misery and hatred. They shall suffer through the pain and evil brought by their forbear upon an innocent and gentle man.

Their lives shall bring suffering to themselves and all who come into contact with them. No woman shall love them for themselves because they possess no love. And no heir will be conceived in love.

Cursed be the name of Reynauld! From age to age, this curse will live on and no man shall break it, because I alone hold the key. Only at the seventh generation will there be hope. A male child conceived in love may sever the chain.

★ ★ ★

I looked up from the book, my mind in a ferment. I now understood Sir Edward's determination to find a wife who would love him. I trembled, because I knew I had no love for him. Would I bear a child by him? And would it be born with that same disfiguring mark There was still another page to read.

★ ★ ★

When I have written this, I must do what I have to do. The curse I have made will become more potent if I sacrifice my own life and that of my unborn child. There are many herbs and plants which will help me. I have learned their secrets. I shall close this book and leave it on the table. Then I shall fetch my potion and drink it here; in this room where my gentle Hugh was taken from me. I can see the stain of his blood still clear upon the floor. May it long remain there to show others what has happened.

I have drunk of the potion and a great weariness fills my body. My last words must be of the misery I will bring to my husband and his family.

Unto the seventh generation . . .

* * *

Here the writing tailed off in a spidery fashion and I knew the draught Yasmin had partaken of was doing its work.

I closed the book and held it in my lap. It was quite plain to me that Sir Geoffrey had not dared to destroy it, as he had burned all the rest of Yasmin's possessions. It had been handed down from elder son to elder son so that her memory should remain strongly in their minds.

I stood up slowly and left the room. I knew whither I was bound. I also knew that Yasmin approved of my coming to her room.

I opened the door and, so clear was the tale told in that little book, that I fancied I could see the room exactly as it had been the day she had taken her own life. The bed . . . now empty . . . the stain upon the floor . . . the girl at the table laboriously plying pen to paper . . . and the goblet beside her, a dark liquid swirling within.

I shut the door behind me and stood silent in the middle of the room. I was waiting for Yasmin.

She came across the floor to me and her face was full of grief. I smiled.

"I can bear no love-child!" I whispered. "Surely I cannot be the one?"

Within my head I heard the words:

"It is not your child!"

And I recalled her words of the previous night.

Then what was I doing here, and why had she shown herself to me? I must have voiced the words aloud because I saw her shake her head as she replied:

"I shall make it known when the time is ripe."

"Is it peace you want, Yasmin?" I asked. "Are you tired of this persecution you have brought to the family?" But she would not answer me, although I knew instinctively that this was what she longed for.

I clasped the book to my breast and looked down again at that mark on the floor. Suddenly I knew I was alone again.

I determined to show my husband what I had found and went boldly back to his study, there to await his arrival. I heard his footsteps in the hall within the hour, and called out to him. He threw open the door, frowning.

"Elaine! What do you do here?"

"I came to seek a book," I lied. "And I found this." I held up the diary. He took some quick strides towards me and then snatched the volume out of my hands.

"How dare you pry!" he accused. "How dare you read such things!"

I was unafraid of his anger. Instead, I pointed to a chair and suggested he should sit down. To my surprise, he agreed.

"Edward," this was the first time I had used his name, and my cheeks reddened. "I understand a great deal now that I have seen this sad record. But there is much left untold." I explained the tales I had heard of Yasmin's death and asked where she had been buried.

He seemed reluctant to tell me, but I remained adamant. Finally he shrugged.

"You are more curious than those who came before you," he commented. "I believe you to be the first to have read this tale. My ancestor, Sir Geoffrey, took this book and hid it so that none but the male members of the family should set eyes upon it. And so it has been throughout the years. When the elder son comes of age, the book is taken out and shown to him, so that he may know exactly why the family is cursed. And the full tale is told. It has never passed beyond these walls and all you hear from outside is the result of years of legend built up from speculation and odd glimmers of the truth."

"I had heard that Yasmin and Hugh were lovers," I admitted. "But I did not know of this. Where was she buried?"

"Sir Geoffrey refused to place her in the vault, and it is told that he alone knew where she had been laid to rest. My grandfather believed it to have been a hidden grave somewhere in the churchyard, but the earth and turf was replaced so carefully that none have found it. Trees and bushes must now have overgrown the place."

"But your mark!" I said, and then lowered my eyes as his finger touched the ugly red crescent.

"This came with the first child born after Yasmin's death. They found her lying on the floor of that room upstairs. She had swallowed poison, as you have read. Sir Geoffrey lost no time in remarrying. He brought a gentle bride from an estate near Exeter and she bore him a son. Upon his face, red and raw like my own, was this huge mark. And it has passed down throughout the generations."

"And you are the seventh generation?" I asked.

"I am. The child you will bear me must break this curse. When born . . . if conceived in love . . . his face will be free of the crescent."

My eyes had not left his face. He rose from his chair and came over to me. Suddenly he sank on to the floor beside me and put his head in my lap.

I clenched my fists, trying to still their trembling of dislike. Then he raised his eyes to my face and his arms slid round my waist, tight and hurtful.

"Elaine! Elaine! Try to love me!" he begged. "Try to love me so that our child will be conceived in love."

Beyond his head I saw the familiar shape of Yasmin's stuart dress. She was watching us, a cynical smile upon her lips. I have always had a deep compassion for those in trouble and, for a moment, I shared my husband's mental torment. I lowered my gaze to that dark head in my lap and my hands strayed towards it. I soothed him like a child.

He clung to me, and I believe that in that one moment I came nearer to understanding him than during the whole period of our married life together. We were as one, united in our acceptance of destiny. I think that, had he taken me there and then, a child might have been conceived in love; yet it would have been in love born of my compassion.

But he did not take me. He remained crouched upon the floor, his head in my lap, and with my hands in his dark, wiry hair. I wanted to lift this dreadful curse. I longed to rid the house of the torture. Strangely enough, I did not condemn Yasmin for her deed. I wanted her to find peace as well.

At the same time I was unable to rid my mind of my husband's short-comings, and was resolute in my determination to find a means of making him carry out his duty as landlord to his tenants.

In her wish to bring misery to the Reynaulds, Yasmin had decreed that all those with whom they came into contact should also suffer. I wondered whether she had considered carefully before determining this fact, because I did not believe she had truly realized the extent of her curse. The villagers had not hurt her; why then should she have harmed them?

Perhaps this was the reason for her wishing to end the curse. I liked to think this was so. She had shown herself to me and was now using me to end the powerful curse she had placed on the family over a hundred and fifty years beforehand. That is how I reasoned it, and it also provided a sensible explanation for my lack of fear of Yasmin.

I had to help her! And, by helping her, I must help my husband. It was a formidable task, but I was a determined person.

12

URING those summer months I was not unhappy. My life seemed now to have a definite purpose, and I had accepted my position in the Reynauld household. In spite of my efforts to get repairs done to the cottages, my husband refused to spend money on them.

"What about the rent?" I protested angrily. "Surely they are entitled to some return for what they pay you?" He came over to me, his eyes glinting, and I stepped back, slightly afraid.

"They are entitled to nothing . . . nothing!" he told me. "And you will refrain from interfering in matters that are of no concern to you."

I remained silent. But I did not cease my visits to the village. Edward knew nothing of them and we were all very careful that he should not suspect. I called frequently to see Mrs. Post and Gabriel, and took comfort in the old woman's strange sayings. She kept on telling me that 'you be the one' and I found myself agreeing with her.

I was alarmed at the state of her cottage and spoke to Robert about it.

"The whole place looks as if it will fall down at any moment!" I complained. "Surely you could persuade my husband to do something?"

He promised to try, and with that I had to be content. However, I learned later that they almost came to blows over the matter. My husband had met Robert in the village and had been taken into the cottage to see for himself how badly the roof rafters were eaten away, and the precarious state of the tottering chimney above.

Bitter words had been exchanged in front of the villagers and Edward had lost his temper, striking Robert across the face with his whip. I did not learn about this until two days after the event, when Mrs. Post told me the story.

"But Robert said he had been scratched by bushes after his horse had stumbled!"

"Bain't true, maid. Jes' bain't true!"

I had come home and gone straight to

the study where Robert was working. He jumped up at my entrance.

"Why didn't you tell me what happened?" I demanded, running to his side. "He cannot be allowed to treat you so!" Robert's answer had been a wry smile and the sensible advice to me to leave well alone. I had remained there, very close to him, our hands almost touching.

It had been then, I believe, that love had been born.

I shocked Mrs. Jane and the servants by suggesting that I used that small room in the other wing as my own private sitting-room. It had a better view than mine, and I thought that Yasmin would not mind. I had not seen her since the discovery of her little book. At times, I was almost inclined to believe I had dreamed everything; although I was quite unable to explain my accurate search for the book. Something had led me straight to it; I could not deny this.

I went into that room and remained there very quietly, trying to draw Yasmin to me, but she did not come. I knew then that I was being allowed to use the room. Mrs. Jane was very doubtful, shaking her head and telling me that the maids would refuse to cross the threshold.

"In that case, let me have brooms and dusters, and I will clean the place myself."

With eyes almost popping out of her head, Lily accompanied me along the passage towards Yasmin's room, and remained poised for flight whilst I opened its door.

"Come along, Lily," I chided. "There's nothing to be frightened of."

"Ooh I don't know, my lady! I reely don't know!"

However, she came into the room with me and stood almost rigid while I relieved her of the brooms.

"Do you feel cold, Lily?" I asked, as I thew open the windows to let in the warm sun.

"No, my lady."

"Do you feel as though we weren't alone?"

She glanced into every corner and shook her head.

"No, my lady."

"In that case, everything's all right. Come, help me with this latch. The window has been closed for so long that the hinges have rusted."

We cleaned the room and furniture was brought in. Other maids came sheepishly to the door, thrusting their noses inside the room like rabbits creeping from their burrows. Obviously they had come to try for themselves, I told myself with amusement. I knew they would sense nothing, because the room had become pleasantly welcome. Yasmin had haunted it in the past. Now she had gone elsewhere.

However, there was one thing I could not persuade the servants to do, and that was to come into the room when I was not present. They were afraid and, as Lily openly confessed, it was because of Yasmin.

"She bain't here when you're here, my lady. But she be jes' biding her time 'til we come along, then she can snap us up."

I tried to laugh away her fears, but she would not be comforted.

It became my custom to sit in the window overlooking the garden during the warm summer evenings, and Edward always looked up, should he be passing. Our relationship had not changed very much. I found myself more tolerant of his outbursts, although I could never rid myself of the deep shame I felt at his refusal to help his tenants. Somehow I felt personally responsible for them. I even caught myself wondering if there were not a trace of madness in some of his actions.

I did my best to respond to his love-making, because I had come to the conclusion that the sooner a boy was born, the more at ease should we all be. Yet I found something within me resisting. I could answer animal passion with some degree of reciprocation, but I felt no deep love for this man who shared the act with me. As time passed, I felt his eyes on me, and knew what he was thinking, although he never expressed his thoughts in words. He knew as well as I did that I had not conceived.

I was conscious also of glances from Robert Polkerris. Often I had to bite back my tongue in order to prevent my impulse to tell him that still there was no child. Somehow it seemed terribly important that I should not have to bear Edward's son. Then again, I would long for the whole thing to be accomplished and the baby lying in my arms.

I would often lie awake at night, listening to the slow breathing on the pillow beside me, and ask myself whether I truly wanted Edward's child. A woman in love longs to bear her man a baby . . . but I was not in love with Edward. I pitied him . . . and I despised him for those examples of cruelty.

The summer days waxed and then waned, and there was dew heavy on the grass in the early mornings. Sea mists tended to creep in, and I knew without having to be told that summer was fast drawing to a close. Soon the gales and sheet-like rain of winter would envelop this wild bay, and my mind turned again and again to those humble, leaking village dwellings.

I had known for some time that minor repairs had been carried out to these homes, but had formed no idea as to the person's identity. I realize now how very stupid I must have been, because the solution was so simple.

Fortunately, neither the repairs nor the person responsible for them were noticeable to Edward.

One early September morning, Lily came running to my sitting-room, pounding on the door with her fist in her haste to attract my attention.

"My lady, I come to tell you that Gabby Post's been up to say his Ma been took bad again. Mrs. Jane be in the still-room busy getting things ready."

"I'll come at once," I replied, because I felt a deep affection for old Mrs. Post. I could not help smiling as I left the room, because Lily offered to remain and tidy it for me. Plainly she had forgotten her fear of Yasmin's 'auntings' as she called them.

"I'll bring your shawl, my lady," she called after me as I hurried towards the staircase. I found Mrs. Jane busy packing a basket, and shaking her head sadly.

"Let's be hoping this isn't the end," she said. "Poor old Mrs. Post gets bad every year this time. I reckon 'tis to do with they mists from the sea and they leaking houses." She lifted the white napkin over the basket and I peered inside. "Gabby says he's given his Ma six middling pills of cobwebs for her ague, but I reckon she needs a plaster of treacle and soot put to the wrists as well. Then he's given her a silk bag with two pennyworth of tarred twine to put on the spot where the rheumatics hurt, but she'd do better to have this rubbed on it." She indicated a bottle and I asked what was in it. "White wine vinegar, turpentine, three egg whites and some alum the size of a nutmeg. My grandfather always swore by it."

I picked up the basket and left the house. When I reached the village I saw the children playing in the dirt of the lane as usual, and waved to them. They clamoured around me, begging to see if I had brought any sweet-meats. Then I went inside the cottage.

To my surprise, another man was present with Gabriel. It was some time before I was able to make him out in the dim interior, and then I recognized Robert Polkerris. He came to me at once, took the basket from me and laid it on a corner of the hob. The fire, I noticed, was out. He saw the direction of my eyes and said:

"I have sent one of the children for firewood. Gabriel's been up all night with his Mother."

The invalid was lying in the narrow, bunk-like bed which was set into the far wall. A fleecy blanket from the Hall covered her. I took her hands and held them tightly, asking how she felt.

"'Tis they rheumaticks, my lover, and that there ague."

I could see that she was far from well.

"Mrs. Jane has packed broth and medicines for you," I said, starting towards the fireplace. "I'll get them for you; then you might like me to rub your sore places?"

"You be a good little maid," she said, and then a paroxysm of coughing seized her. I supported her so that she could breathe more easily while the attack lasted, and then laid her back in the bed.

While I rubbed her back and shoulders I sent the men from the cottage. Half an hour later the fire had been relit and the pan of broth Mrs. Jane had sent was steaming and bubbling as it swung from the chain over the flames. Mrs. Post was looking far easier now that her bed had been tidied and her aching limbs rubbed and soothed. I had tied the treacle plasters around her thin wrists and then pulled the sleeve of her ragged nightgown down over them. I had a spare nightgown . . . Edward had ordered far too many from that seamstress in Bodmin.

I had noticed hammering but had not paid much attention to it whilst I was feeding Mrs. Post from a bowl of hot broth. I now looked up and saw that Robert was helping Gabriel to replace a badly splintered panel in the front entrance door. My patient smiled.

"He's a good boy, that one. Don't know what we'd have done without him. Risks your man's fury by coming here to help us."

"Gabriel?" I asked, puzzled.

"Lawks, no, my lover. Robert be the man."

Robert Polkerris! Why had I not realized this before? I wondered, and then knew how stupid I had been. I had heard whispers in the village, but the inhabitants had not trusted me sufficiently to share the entire secret with me. I felt a little sad and then told myself that it was only natural to be suspicious . . . especially as I was closer than anyone else to the man they all hated. And I had accused Robert of using the money for his own means.

I was deeply ashamed of my thoughtlessness.

"I didn't realize," I said in a weak voice to Mrs. Post.

"Of course you didn't. Yet who else but he could help us, eh? He knows what's wanted, and he has the money."

"Surely he isn't stealing it from my husband?" I asked, aghast, because I knew what Edward might do should he discover a thief.

"Bless you, no! Robert Polkerris bain't no thief! He uses what little money he gets for working at the Hall. Takes home just enough for living and the rest he spends on the likes of we."

I looked again at Robert, silhouetted in the open doorway, and the still strong September sunshine showed up the faded patches in his clothes. He sensed my interest, because he turned to look at me. Although I knew he could not see me all that well, I lowered my gaze, afraid lest he should see my shame.

Throughout the remainder of the time I spent with the Posts, I was acutely conscious of Robert Polkerris. I wanted to touch him; even to brush close to him would have satisfied my urge for his nearness. But I could remain no longer. Smiling at the invalid, I rose to my feet.

"I will come and see you tomorrow," I promised. "In the meantime, I will send one of the maids with some things you might find useful." The swollen hands sought mine and I held them tenderly.

"God bless you, my lady!"

A lump rose in my throat as I turned away to pick up my basket from the window sill where it now rested. I smiled at Gabriel and told him not to worry. Then I left the cottage. Robert accompanied me to the door where I paused, my eyes intent on a centipede which was bustling its legged way across the uneven stone flag.

"Thank you for coming, my lily maid," Robert murmured. I could not bring myself to answer, because I knew that he might read my thoughts in my eyes and tone. I think I must have muttered something, then I fled down the tiny path and into the lane leading back to the Hall.

My feet started to lag and I looked back at the huddled dwellings. Of so much had I accused him! Impulsive, accepting everything at face value . . . was there no end to my stupidity? I then did something which I was to come to regret for the remainder of my life at the Hall. I made up my mind to wait for Robert.

I found a warm dip between the dunes, not far from the lane along which I knew he must come in order to reach Reynauld Hall. I sat down, my arms around my knees, and watched the sand rise and fall as the breeze gusted it between the marran grass.

I did not have long to wait. I heard whistling and then the inching of heavy feet. He sounded happy. I felt my heart bound within my breast. He came into sight and paused before me, smiling. I stood up. He walked towards me.

Oh the foolishness of planned actions! I had told myself exactly what I must say to him; exactly what to do. Intention and action rarely coincide. I stumbled into his arms, murmuring his name, while he laughingly caught me to him whispering against my mouth:

"My Lily maid of Astolat!"

I do not know how long we stood there. Time seemed non-existent in the frantic need to give of oneself. I cannot even recall whether people passed us, although I believe that Edward must have ridden near. I can speak of it now, because the fear has passed. I have often wondered why he did not kill Robert, for such action would have solved his problem for ever. Perhaps it was a vicious streak within his mind that prompted him to take the course he chose? I know he planned to hurt me. I know he wished to part us. I sincerely believe that he dared not kill for fear I should kill myself and rob him once again of that male child.

I do not know what transpired between the two men when they met on our return. Robert has never spoken of that time. Over the years I have managed to fit together small pieces of the puzzle, and I believe this is what must have happened. My husband threatened Robert with my own life. It was as simple as that. He sincerely believed that, by leaving the Hall and everything it meant to him, he would be saving me from punishment . . . and death.

Naturally I did not escape all my husband's wrath. For three days he kept me locked in my bedchamber, refusing to give any reason for such an act. Lily was forbidden to bring me my food, lest she should tell me what had happened. Instead, Edward himself collected the trays from Mrs. Jane who brought them as far as the top of the staircase before handing them over to him.

I longed to ask after Mrs. Post, yet dared not do so. For three days and nights I suffered agonies of mental torment as I wondered what had been happening during my imprisonment.

On the morning of the fourth day, Edward unlocked the door and told me that I was free to resume my normal activities. When I walked past him, he caught my arm and said:

"I am warning you, Elaine, and I advise you to take good heed of my words. Have nothing further to do with Robert Polkerris."

I pretended ignorance, although my mind seethed with anxiety. What had he learned? What had he done to Robert?

"Where . . . where is he?" I asked in a forced tone.

"He has been dismissed. Should he return here, for any reason at all, I shall have no hesitation in shooting him as a trespasser."

"What has he done?" I demanded, my eyes fierce.

"Displeased me greatly. In future, I shall attend to the management of my own estate and affairs. It seems that history tends to repeat itself at times." Then he left me to ponder his words.

I knew then that he must have suspected the love between myself and Robert.

I rang for Mrs. Jane and asked at once if there was any news of Mrs. Post. Her words were reassuring.

"And Mr. Polkerris?" I added, my eyes

on the closed door. She leaned closer and lowered her voice.

"He left three days ago, my lady. We been ordered not to speak of him again. But . . . " her eyes sought that stolid door . . . "if news comes to us, like as not we'll be letting your ladyship know?"

And with that promise I had to be content.

13

IT may have been my fancy, but the weather seemed to change for the worst immediately after Robert's departure. The heat faded from the sun, the icy chill from the shrouding sea mists seemed to reach to the bone, and the moan of the wind around the house never completely died away. It was as if some giants stood without, whispering amongst themselves. Inside the building, shutters creaked, draughts howled under doors, candle flames contorted themselves in weird dances as they bent before these gusts like willows in the marsh. Huge logs burned in the enormous grates, yet their heat appeared to dissipate up the wide chimneys, leaving the rooms cold and comfortless. If I stood before one to warm my hands, my face burned unpleasantly, while my back shivered.

The house was strangely quiet without Robert Polkerris. Each time I passed the closed door of my husband's study,

I half-expected the latch to lift and the door to swing wide. Occasionally I ventured into the room and stood looking down at the desk where he had worked. I longed for news of him, but none was forthcoming, in spite of the promises made to me by my faithful Mrs. Jane.

I went to the village where I was greeted enthusiastically. I made tentative enquiries concerning Robert's whereabouts and was rewarded by tightly closed lips. I cannot describe the depth of my despair! I had thought I had won the confidence of these good people, yet they were unprepared to share this one secret with me. Plainly I was not to be trusted.

I was glad to find Mrs. Post well on the way to recovery, although she complained that the damp autumn weather made her limbs and bones ache. She seldom left her chair by the fire, meagre though it was. I told Gabriel to come to the house and fetch some of our own winter fuel from the woodpile, but he shook his head. And I knew he dared not risk Edward's wrath. I promised to speak to him on the matter but Gabriel shook his head.

Naturally Edward would have none of my plan. I had asked if the villagers might be allowed some extra firewood and the sound of his hand striking the dining table between us startled me.

"Lazy good-for-nothings! Let them find their own fuel! They have the sea at their doors. Why should we provide timber for burning when they have natural resources from which to take their choice?" He stared at my bewildered face in exasperation. "You're not their wet-nurse! Let them collect driftwood and seaweed! And the dried dung of their own animals. I'll hear no more on this matter. And you'll be well advised yourself to keep away from the village."

I said no more, for fear I should lose my temper. It seemed to me that, whichever method I chose, there was no way in which I could help the villagers. Life was not fair, I decided. Edward takes the rent due to him, yet gives nothing in return. He owned the land, the cottages and the cottagers themselves. Some of the men worked in the tin mine while others struggled to find a living from the sea. They were completely dependent on him for food and lodging. If any dared to displease him, then he turned them from their homes. They dared not raise their voices too high in protest.

Edward was a man without compassion. As long as his own life was unaffected, the villagers were as expendable as worn-out clothing.

Those weeks following Robert's departure were indescribably lonely, and incomparable even to my first months at Mrs. Crane's. I had been much younger then and alone in the world, yet there seemed now to be a bottomless depth to the intense unhappiness I was experiencing. There must have been more than one reason for this; cumulatively, they became an overwhelming despair. At times I found myself wondering whether it might be easier to end it all . . .

The wide bay with its grey, curling sea and the wind buffeting me while I trod those clean, yellow sands; was I the only being alive in the world? Two gulls rising and falling on the thermals from the land; their grey wings outstretched, seemingly to touch the lowering clouds; the solitary mizzen mast of a far distant boat that battled through the choppy water; surely they called to me to join them? The eerie cry from above my head as the yellow beak of one of the gulls opened ... cark-cark-cark-cark ... they say that the souls of the dead lost at sea live on anew in these birds. Should I take the step to join them? It would be so easy just to walk out into those slate grey waters until they closed over my head ...

In the cold of the autumn the house seemed to take on a mood of foreboding. I often stood beyond the marsh and stared at it. I had the ridiculous feeling that it was trying to tell me something, and I am sure I heard a voice in the wind cry out: Go! Go!

I missed Robert Polkerris but I think I missed Yasmin more. From my arrival she had become part of me; I had associated myself with her in some way, and now I felt less than whole. She had shown me the way to her diary, and then had left me. Yet I was certain in my own mind that her purpose in showing herself to me was still not fully accomplished. All my efforts to bring her to me again failed. I must be patient.

All thoughts of Yasmin and Robert Polkerris slipped from my mind the day I knew I was to bear Edward a child. I was surprised, for I had not wanted this to happen so soon after my marriage. It would not be a love-child as Edward had desired, and I was afraid what might happen when it was born. Would the gipsy curse show itself again on my son's face? Should I hold in my arms a baby disfigured by the glaring red crescent?

I lay on my bed, weeping bitterly. I wallowed in self-pity and, looking back now at that time, I feel a deep shame for my complete lack of control. The life I led was unnatural. Being so much on my own, I had become obsessed by the great house, my thoughts and fears, the gipsy curse and, above all, the shade of Yasmin. To me she was almost a real person. And I had scorned all those who were superstitious!

Why did Yasmin not come to me? She must do so now that I am pregnant!

I chose my time for telling Edward about his child. I needed him to be in a reasonable frame of mind. I think

I really wanted to keep such news to myself for as long as possible, but I knew that the fact of my condition might probably keep him from my bed. And I hated his lovemaking! I hated the manner in which he forced himself upon me; almost as if it were a private tussle between us, as he tried to encourage my responses. There was no affection in the act; this was the reason for my dislike. I must admit that, at times, his animal passion had succeeded in arousing within me some similar response, yet this was infrequent. I shuddered at his touch. I trembled within his arms. I felt as though I were being suffocated when the weight of his heavy body pressed me into the feather mattress beneath us both. Often I cried out in pain, although I soon learned to bite my lips against such outcries. They seemed only to intensify his own passion and I knew that he delighted in hurting me.

We had finished our evening meal when I told him. His chair scraped across the floor as he pushed it back, then he was by my side, his arms about my waist and his dark head buried in my lap. He uttered strange sounds and, looking down, I saw to my disgust that he was weeping.

It was all I could do not to recoil with revulsion. Not to this day have I forgotten the yellow light from the candelabra falling on his thick, wiry hair, the gleam of sweat on the broad forehead and the glitter of tears in those night-dark eyes that eventually looked up at me before he pulled my face down to his, eagerly seeking my lips.

"I knew you would not fail me!" he whispered. "I knew you would be the one to bear a male child!"

Mercifully, I fainted. My condition had subjected me to strange dizzinesses and nausea, but my husband's very proximity and words had proved too much for me. When I regained consciousness, I found myself lying on my bed with Lily rubbing my hands between hers.

"Oh, my lady!" she breathed in relief. "You didn't half give us a turn! Are you feeling better? The Master's sent for the doctor from Camelford, and he says you're to lie here until he arrives."

I felt rather foolish and struggled to sit up.

"I'm perfectly all right, thank you, Lily." Her gentle hands pressed me back into the pillows. "I don't need any doctor."

"You'll just have to stay there, my lady. Like it was with Lady Julia and Lady Janet. Would have his way and got the doctor for them both. But you be better than they?" she finished, raising her eyebrows enquiringly.

"I am quite fit and well, Lily."

"Oh, I'm so glad! The others were poorly most of the time, on and off, so to speak, so the Master gets worried."

I decided to allow myself a pampering and meekly lifted my arms when Lily brought the warmed night-shift from beside the fire. Soon I was lying back against the pillows, watching the firelight flicker on the walls. I was drowsy and closed my eyes momentarily. When I reopened them, she was standing beside the bed.

"Yasmin!" I whispered and smiled at her. Her hands were folded in front of her, reminding me strangely of the way

230

in which Mrs. Jane stood whilst waiting for her orders. "Why have you come?"

I listened for her words inside my head, but heard none. I did not take my eyes from her. Her own, I saw, were dark green and rather like the pools left between the rocks by the outgoing tide. I found my gaze riveted. I watched as she moved from my side and went to the chair which Lily had placed at the foot of the bed. Then she sat down and her hands sank on to her lap. I distinctly heard the rustle of silk as the fabric moved.

My eyelids were very heavy . . .

"I will look after you," said Yasmin's voice just before I fell asleep.

When I awoke the following morning, a gale roared and rattled around the house. I lay still, listening to the strange noises made by the wind, and then turned my head towards the window where the rain beat in silver-grey sheets. It was a terrible day and one best spent in bed, I thought. There was no real need for me to get up, especially if the doctor should arrive from Camelford.

I took an immediate liking to portly

Dr. Bull. His cheerful red face and friendly manner acted like a tonic, which was just what I needed to jolt me out of my present mood. Perched on the side of the four-poster, with his short legs barely reaching the floor, he chatted to me.

"I expect you'll find the winters here a little bleak to start with," he commented, jerking his head in the direction of the wild weather beyond the window. "The gale'll soon blow itself out. And it doesn't blow like this throughout the entire winter, you know! We have our good days as well. Then I reckon you won't be knowing the difference between the seasons, what with the sun out and the air warm. Not as warm as summer, of course, but warm enough to make you wonder where winter went to in such a hurry. All the same, when it blows, 'tis best to keep indoors, because the Atlantic's a rough and cruel place when she's angered and her gales rip in from the sea, uprooting trees and blowing in windows." He beamed at me and patted my hand. "I don't see why you need stay in bed. Just a slight dizzy turn, but you're a strong young woman." His smile faded as he added, rather indiscreetly, I thought: "Not like your two predecessors. The faintest puff of wind would have blown them over. Not surprising they were unfit for child-bearing." He stood up. "Now I'll go down to your husband who will be wearing out the carpet with his anxious pacings."

I was sorry when he had left the room. I was sleepy and decided to doze before getting out of bed. However, I had not closed my eyes for long before Edward came into the room and stood by the bed. The relief on his face had wiped away some of the harsher lines.

"You are quite fit, I believe," he said. "Doctor Bull tells me that you may get up. I'd prefer you to stay in bed for the rest of the day, just in case."

I laughed and propped myself on one elbow.

"But I am perfectly fit, if just a little sleepy."

"Nevertheless, you'll do as I say and stay in bed. Lily can bring you your meals. In spite of the weather, I must go to the mine for a few hours. Will you be all right on your own?"

"Of course I will!"

His face showed his reluctance to leave me and I laughed again.

"Edward, there's *nothing* wrong with me!" I told him. "I'm barely three months pregnant, and there are many still left to go. I hope you're not going to treat me like an invalid throughout that time?"

He knelt beside me and seized my hands.

"Elaine, listen to me! I have already lost two sons and could not bear losing a third. I shall cherish and care for you! You are my very life . . . and hope."

He stood up and bent over me, giving me a swift kiss. Then he had gone. A tinkling laugh filled the room, and I turned my head quickly. Yasmin stood by the window, her hands on the heavy curtains, and she was laughing, as at some enormous joke. I was filled with a sudden anger.

"Oh, for goodness sake!" I called out. "Cannot you leave me in peace?"

The smile left her face and she came across to me, staring down at me, her eyes suddenly dark green and very hard.

"I have not finished with him yet!"

her voice drummed within my head. I clapped my hands over my ears and turned from her. When eventually I peeped round again she had gone.

I was awoken around midday by the bursting open of my door. I jerked upright, to see Lily standing beside me, wringing her hands and with tears pouring down her cheeks.

"Oh Miss! My Lady! Something dreadful's happened! It was the wind and they there rafters in the cottage. Mrs. Post's been killed."

"Killed? How?"

"Oh, Miss, please can you come? They say Gabby's in a dreadful way, rantin' and ravin' about the Master and how he'll kill him! Oh Miss, you *must* go to him! You're the only one who can help him."

All thoughts for my own health left me. I flung back the bedding and put my feet to the ground, ordering Lily to bring my clothes and a warm cloak. She scurried to obey, talking and weeping all the time.

"Young Pauley brought the news. Says Mrs. Post was awful bad when they got her out. In all that there rain, too!"

I scrambled into my clothes and then wrapped my cloak about my shoulders and head. I didn't think of Edward and what he might say, should he learn of my departure from the house. The thought uppermost in my mind was for Gabriel and the grief caused by this terrible accident.

Lily and I almost ran to the village. The gale had abated, but a strong wind still blew in from the sea, forcing us to walk with our heads down, and bent nearly double. When we drew near the village, the spume beat into our hair as it was lifted high above the dunes.

A small crowd had gathered outside the remains of the Posts' home. Women turned at my coming and many had their aprons at their eyes, dabbing away the tears. They stepped aside and I walked up to the front entrance where I could see the huddled figure of Gabriel. He was soaked to the skin as he crouched beside the shrouded body of his dead mother. Someone had brought an old bedspread to cover that broken body, but he had retained hold of the withered hand, pressing it against his chest. I touched his shoulder.

"Gabriel, I'm so sorry," I said gently. His ravished face turned to mine and there was fire and madness in his tortured eyes.

"He killed her!" he whispered. "Killed her! Robert Polkerris said the chimney was unsafe. He did nothing to repair it, and then the wind brought it crashing through the rotten rafters as she sat by the fire this morning."

I crouched beside the boy, my arms about him, and drew him tightly against me, as I would have done a small child.

"It was an accident, Gabriel. An accident!"

"It were all the Master's fault, my lady," someone piped up from behind me. "That there chimney been bad for years. Should have been took down and put up again like new so's it couldn't crush they rotten rafters inside the place."

"Is there anywhere we can take Mrs. Post" I asked, searching the sea of faces around me. "Will one of you take her and Gabriel?"

"We will, my lady." Two elderly men

walked through the throng and came up to us. "We'll have her laid out in our parlour. Young Gabby can sleep in our place."

"He killed her! He killed her!" Gabriel wept, that cold hand still clutched against him. I looked round at the men behind me.

"You must take her now," I said gently.

"He wouldn't have us touch her afore you came, Missis."

"Gabby, you must let them take Ma where she'll be out of this rain and wind." The boy hesitated. "It isn't right to leave her lying here; you know that, don't you, Gabby?" I spoke softly, using the diminutive. "Come, let me help you." I reached for the dead woman's hand and tucked it beneath the shrouding bedspread. Then I helped Gabriel to his feet.

The men lifted the body and walked before us across the street, towards one of the other cottages. Mrs. Post was so small and frail that they were able to carry her with ease. As they went, a corner of her red shawl slipped out and swung to and fro, Gabriel's eyes watched it.

I was almost dropping with exhaustion when Lily helped me home. It had taken all my diplomacy and persuasion to convince the grieving boy that his mother should be prepared for burial and that he, too, should rest. I left everything in the hands of the rector who had come hurrying from his home two miles away. He was in charge of three villages and could not always be on hand when required. He took immediate charge of the situation, lifting a great load from my shoulders, and I hoped that his presence might bring comfort and peace to Gabriel's stricken mind. I preferred not to think of the boy's accusations against my husband. Everything he had said had been true. It was Edward's responsibility to provide his tenants with fit habitation. If a repair was needed, then it should have been carried out. In my mind's eye, I could see old Mrs. Post sitting in her chair beside the fire, her gnarled hands seeking its warmth. Suddenly, a fierce crack and crumbling noise above her head . . . perhaps she had had time to look up as the chimney came crashing through the roof, ripping the worm-eaten rafters and falling upon her . . . then the frantic pulling away of debris as Gabriel struggled to reach her, his voice hoarse with fear. The final smile as she looked up at her son for the last time . . . then nothing . . . but darkness . . .

Yes, his was the right to accuse. My husband's lack of interest and negligence had brought grief and sorrow to an already stricken village. This time there was nothing I could do to alleviate the pain.

To my horror, when I reached the house with Lily, I found that Edward had already returned. His voice bellowed to me when I passed the open door to his study. I hesitated, while Lily's terrified eyes sought mine. I patted her hand and told her to take my wet and dirty cloak upstairs. Then I raised my head determinedly and went into the study.

"Why are you not in bed?" Edward roared, but he did not get up from the chair in which he was sprawled. He winced as he made a slight movement.

"Are you in pain?" I asked.

"Never mind me. Where have you been? Did I not give you express orders to remain in bed? How dare you go out in such weather! Are you deliberately trying to kill my son?"

I stood and watched him while he writhed in the chair. He had hurt himself, that was quite plain, and I knew he could not strike me for disobedience. I told him what had happened, watching his face for reaction.

"I was going to pull down the place in the spring," he commented in a cold voice. "Nature has saved me the trouble."

"Is that all you can say?" I demanded furiously. "Have you no pity for the woman killed, or grief for her son?"

"They are dirt and useless, I should have turned them out next spring."

My face was filled with loathing. I came to his chair and stared down at him, my knuckles showing white as I gripped the wooden arm.

"What is Life to you? Is it so insignificant that it can be wiped away like the ripples of the water upon the sand out there?" I waved my hand towards the window. "Does a human soul count for nothing?"

"Oh, go away!" he muttered. "I am not in the mood for sermonizing."

I put my hand on his shoulder and he cried out in pain.

"Damn you, woman! Let me go!" he roared.

"You are hurt. How did it happen?"

"My mare slipped on the greasy ground and we fell. She rolled on top of me, bruising my shoulder."

"Are any bones broken?" I felt with the tips of my fingers and he groaned.

"I doubt it. We Reynaulds are of strong stock." His eyes flickered to mine. "Remember that, Elaine. The child you must bear me is to be strong."

"The mare? Did she hurt herself?"

"A strained fetlock, I think. She'll be right enough in a few days. I had Parker apply liniment and hot bandages."

I uttered a derisory snort as I accused:

"You take care of your horses, but you treat your tenants like vermin." I placed both hands on my abdomen. "I think I can see why your previous wives were loathe to bring a child to full term.

Had I the courage, I would destroy as you destroy!"

I turned on my heels and left the room, slamming the door with all my might while he bellowed after me:

"You kill that child and I'll strangle you with my own hands!"

His threats meant nothing. I had sufficient confidence in my own position to know that he would risk little in order to bring my child to full term. Afterwards . . . that was a different matter. Would he dispose of me? I wondered, and shuddered. But common sense soon asserted itself. I was indispensible to the welfare of the heir. He needed a mother, and therefore my safety in this house was assured.

When I reached my own room, the thought came to me:

If your child should be a girl?

14

BECAUSE of his badly bruised shoulder, Edward was obliged to remain in bed for a few days. He was a churlish patient and I informed him that I would not be spoken to in the manner he was now using. He then retorted by telling me that he was still Master of the house, and that he would do as he wanted. I merely nodded and then left him severely alone.

I did not tell him about Mrs. Post's funeral. I decided it would be better for him to learn after the event. I think I was afraid that he might find some means of keeping me away from the village.

It was a dull but dry morning when I joined the long line of sorrowing mourners behind the cheap coffin. Black dresses and bands had been resurrected from the bottom of clothes chests, and every head was bent. Even the children remained silent and unprotesting as they clutched the hands of their parents on their way through the dunes towards the tiny church. My eyes sought Gabriel; that solitary figure stumbling behind the coffin as it was carried on the shoulders of four young men.

I listened to the rector's droning monotone, and then joined the procession to the side of that ugly scar in the churchyard. Women sobbed and children whimpered. The coffin vanished from sight beneath the surface of the ground. Gabriel fell to his knees and pressed his hands over his face.

I made a move to join him but a hand on my elbow spun me round. My eyes widened as they alighted on the face of Robert Polkerris.

"Robert!" I breathed. "I did not know that you had come!"

"Leave him be, my lady," he advised, indicating Gabriel. "Leave him to his sorrow." I stood looking at the boy, wanting to comfort him, yet recognizing the wisdom of Robert's words. The villagers passed by, their interested gaze alighting on us both and then being hastily averted. Soon we were alone in the churchyard, save for that solitary, mourning figure.

"Come, I want to talk to you," Robert said, his hand guiding me towards the lych-gate. "Is your husband near?"

"No." I told him what had happened and Robert was relieved. "Why have you come today?"

"Mrs. Post was a dearly loved friend. I wished to pay my last respects."

"Did you not fear my husband's wrath?" I asked, "I have heard whispers amongst the villagers that he would kill you, should you dare to come back."

"Very true. However, as you have told me yourself, I have no cause for fear today." His eyes became soft. "Besides, I have stayed away long enough. I wanted so much to see you . . . to hold your hand again . . . to speak with you. Are you keeping well. You look tired." His gaze flickered over me and I blushed.

"I am well. I . . . " but I found myself unable to tell him.

"You are with child, I know."

"How?"

"Word travels fast in these areas. Doctor Bull is a good friend of mine."

"I see."

He looked out across the sea at the horizon and his voice was sad.

"Had it not been for the child, I think I would have asked you to come with me today. I have found these weeks unbearable."

"I also," I choked, my throat constricted. His hand tightened on mine and I leaned closer to him.

"But it shall not be. Not now." He seemed to pull himself together, and moved his body away from mine. A thin smile lingered on his lips. "Destiny has proved too much for us both. Would that it had been I who had found you in London! 'Tis too late now for recriminations. You will bear your husband a son and the curse will be broken. Life for everyone on the Reynauld estate will be happy again. After all these years . . . through the agency of a young and very beautiful women . . . " he pulled away his hand and bowed to me. "I can say no more but bid you good day, my lady."

"Please don't go!" I called out after him. "Robert . . . Please!" But I knew it

247

was useless. He had made up his mind that nothing but unhappiness could come of our prolonging the agony of being together. My words reached his ears, for he was but a short way off, yet he refused to turn round. I was glad of his strength. I was weak . . . weak . . .

My eyes were red when I went into Edward's room at his command. He stared at me in a sneering manner and said:

"You are too soft with people, but it is a good thing in a mother. I pray that you will not spoil our son by over-pampering. I shall be around to see that he is brought up as a son should be reared."

I did not explain that half my unhappiness was at Mrs. Post's passing, and the rest for the loss of my own future.

Because his shoulder pained him more at night, Edward asked me to leave ajar the communicating door between our rooms. He hoped, I believe, that I would hear his moans and come to comfort him. But this I steadfastly refused to do. Naturally such bruising would cause pain, but there was no need to act like a spoiled child! I was a light sleeper, in any case, and I knew that the sounds of his restlessness would probably keep me awake long into the early hours.

How bitterly I resented those moans and groans! How selfish and thoughtless Edward was! I turned over in bed and pulled up the sheets to my ears, trying to block out the sounds. Suddenly I stiffened, and then raised my head to listen more carefully.

The noises had altered and I could have sworn that I heard a footstep in the other room.

Was he out of bed? If so, why then had the moaning in his sleep not ceased?

I was intrigued, and propped myself on my elbow. A floorboard creaked and I knew that someone else was in Edward's bedroom. I tossed back the bed clothes and put my feet on the carpet, then I slipped noiselessly through the open doorways between our two rooms. A quick glance into the moonlit dressing-room as I passed showed me that it was empty. Then I reached Edward's bedroom and saw the figure of a man standing at the foot of the bed.

I don't know to this day whether I saw the glint of the knife in his hand, or whether I knew instinctively what he had come to do, but I did not hesitate. I covered the floor between the door and the bed in a couple of bounds, flinging myself down on top of Edward's sleeping body. He uttered a loud cry as I jarred his shoulder.

"No! No!" I cried out to the intruder. "You cannot get even this way."

My intuition had told me the identity of the intruder, and now the moon was silhouetting his upright figure. It was Gabriel Post.

"Get away from there, my lady!" he ordered in a harsh whisper. "Get away lest I harm you."

Edward was struggling to sit up but I was still sprawled across him. I cannot think what had prompted me to save my husband from certain death. I did not love him. I did not even like him! The world would have been a better place without him. Yet there I was, protecting him with my own life!

"Mistress Elaine." Gabriel pleaded, his

hand reaching, but not touching my shoulder.

"No, Gabriel, no! This will not right the wrong he did your mother! You cannot take the law into your own hands like this!"

"Gabriel Post!" Edward's voice was like a long-drawn hiss in my ear. "Ring for the servants . . . quickly, Elaine!"

"Please Gabby! *Please* go!" I begged and started to get to my feet. Because I had succeeded in staying the blow, I knew it would need far more courage to spur himself into inflicting it for the second time. I was in the room and the intended victim was awake. I saw Gabriel hesitate, and stood close to him, my hand seeking the knife. Cold steel chilled my flesh and I felt the relaxation of his grip when I took it away from him. Then it fell on to the soft carpet without a sound.

"Go now, Gabby!" I advised in a soft voice. "While there is still time . . . go! Forget all thoughts of revenge. He isn't worth the forfeiture of your own life."

With a strangled cry of despair. Gabriel rushed from the room.

"After him, girl! Don't let the blackguard escape!" Edward roared, but I simply shut the door and returned to the bed, sitting down heavily upon it, and holding my head in my hands as the room started to spin around me. From a great distance I heard the striking of a tinder against the box, then I saw the sputter of the bedside candle Edward had lit. I breathed deeply, trying to ward off my dizziness. I felt his good arm come round me and I leaned against him.

"Damn you, woman!" he muttered angrily, "I could have summoned the servants, yet you have to suffer a fit of the vapours."

I felt him help me to my feet and then I was being assisted back into my own room . . . by way of detour towards the bell tassel! My head stopped swimming as soon as I was back in my bed with Edward bending over me, his bruised arm resting in his good one.

Then I heard servants being chided for their delay in answering the call, followed by orders for the stable staff to be roused and the horses saddled. I struggled to sit up.

"Where are you going?" I called out to Edward who was in his dressing-room.

"After the rogue, what else? He cannot have gone far. I shall hang him for attempted murder!"

"But your arm!" I protested. "You cannot ride in your condition."

"I can and I will. I shall have him back here by dawn, I promise."

I willed myself to get out of bed but weakness lay heavy upon me. I sank back into the pillows and thought about that distraught would-be assassin. Why had I stayed his hand? Would not it have been better to leave him to complete his mission and slip away again into the darkness, with no one the wiser? Why had I brought Edward's attention to him? From now on, poor Gabriel Post would be a marked man throughout the entire county.

Edward came back into my room and I saw that he was dressed for riding. My heart sank when I saw the heavy pistol hanging from his belt.

"Have mercy on him!" I whispered. "He has done you no harm. Cannot you forget tonight?"

"In the devil's name, I will not! He intended to kill me."

"He doesn't know what he's doing." I continued, impassioned. "His mind is too full of grief at his mother's death. I beg you, Edward, show him compassion for my sake!"

"You women are too soft. The rogue must get his due." He bent over me and dropped an embarrassed kiss on my forehead. "I shall always remember how you saved me, my dear."

Then he had gone.

I thrust my knuckles into my mouth to stifle a cry. I had bungled everything! Now Gabriel was a hunted man. Why, oh why, had I not allowed him to finish his self-imposed task?

From outside the house I heard shouting and saw the reflection of lamps as the male servants joined their Master. I heard too, his voice shouting orders, and I trembled for that poor, lost soul . . . Gabriel Post.

I heard the wind as it swirled around the grey stone building, and I saw the arc of the moon travel across my window. I strained my ears, yet could hear nothing from outside. My mind accompanied that pathetic, fleeing creature, and I closed my eyes in prayer that he should not be apprehended.

I think I must have dozed for a short while, because I suddenly awoke to hear shouts of fear and to see a great red light reflected against the far wall of my room. I sat up to listen. Then I left my bed and went to the window to look out, expecting to see my husband's servants gathered on the lawn beneath, with Gabriel fettered in their midst. Instead I saw the white, upturned faces of the female servants. I heard one call out and point at me.

"The mistress! She'll be trapped! She's still in her room!"

Suddenly I knew what had happened. The smell of burning came fierce and acrid to my nostrils. I looked to my right and saw the inferno that had been part of the wing in which I now stood. I flung open the window and shouted down to those scared, white, helpless faces:

"I shall come down by the staircase near my sitting-room!"

Then I ran across to the bed, grabbed

the bedspread and flung open my door. At exactly the same time, a male figure burst into the room. We collided and I fell backwards under the onslaught.

"My lady! I thought the servants had brought you out!" It was Gabriel Post. "I wouldn't have harmed a hair of your lovely head."

I could only gasp his name. Then he had lifted me into his strong arms and was running with me down the smoke-filled passage towards a back stairway. I wanted to ask him how he came still to be inside the house, but I knew I must not talk; the smoke was choking us both.

We came to the staircase and went down it. Then Gabriel got lost, for we wandered through passage after passage, meeting walls of flame as we twisted and turned.

"Don't be afeared, little lady," he soothed tenderly. "I'll get us out somehow."

The red flickering in the night sky had drawn the search party back to the house with all haste. When Gabriel burst with me from a narrow side entrance, we saw them galloping up the drive at full speed. The horses neighed in fright before they were reined in; then the men were leaping off their saddles and running towards the waiting servants. The maids and scullions were sobbing hysterically, while Mrs. Jane moved from one to another of them, trying to comfort them.

"Where is my wife?" I heard Edward shout. I tried to call back, but Gabriel's hand fastened tightly over my mouth. He shrank back with me into some sheltering trees.

"She be still in her room!" Lily screamed. "'Tis all my fault! I thought I saw her come out with us! Look!" and I saw her pointing.

"God help us!" Edward's voice rang out. "She's in her sitting-room. There! At the window! Struggling to get out, and the flames behind her! She bears my son!" And he let out a dreadful cry.

I saw him rush for the front entrance and vanish into the house. It was now that Gabriel took his hand from my mouth and carried me across to the waiting servants. Their gaze was riveted to the sitting-room window. My eyes followed theirs and I gasped in sheer horror.

A figure in a night-shift identical to mine . . . with my light brown hair . . . and my features . . . stood calling out for help, her hands raised in despair and supplication.

"But I am *here!*" I breathed. "Who among us is missing?"

"The Mistress! The Mistress! She be safe, oh she be safe!" Mrs. Jane cried out and all faces turned to greet me. "Master Gabby . . . you good, good boy!" She fell on me, weeping, and I patted her shoulder awkwardly.

"Mrs. Jane, are all the girls here?" I asked, my tone urgent.

"Why yes, my lady. 'Twas only yourself who was missing. The Master, he went inside for you, my lady."

"Then *who* is that at my sitting-room window?"

My eyes sought that figure again. The ear-ring glittered in the light of the flames, and the wide mouth was open laughing with joy. Her now dark hair swung about her as she turned to greet the man who entered the room. We all saw it happen. We all saw Yasmin standing at that window. Firelight can play strange tricks on the eyes, but all of us gathered there could not have been mistaken.

Edward's arms were stretched towards Yasmin and I knew that he thought she was I. With a final toss of her black hair, she vanished. Then there came a tremendous roar and sparks leaped hundreds of feet into the sky, showering and spluttering like devil's lights. The roof caved in and the entire wing in which I had my private sitting-room was engulfed in the inferno.

I watched until my eyes smarted. The heat was so intense that we were obliged to retreat farther into the garden. Gabriel stayed with me throughout that night, and I remember saying to him:

"Now you have nothing to fear."

15

THE fire raged for over thirty hours; its heat so intense that no one dared go near the smouldering building for a further twenty-four. Edward had not been seen since that final appearance at the window of my sitting-room. I did not want his body found, although I knew a search would be made as soon as the heat became less intense.

They were very good to me, those simple village folk. Gabriel insisted on carrying me back to the village where a bed by a kitchen fire was speedily prepared for me. I was too exhausted and shocked to enquire the whereabouts of my servants; I knew they would be provided for by friends and relations and I guessed that there probably would be some accommodation available in the tiny rooms above the stables at the Hall. These buildings had escaped the blaze, as had also my husband's horses.

Events proved too much. On the

morning after the fire I was seized with crippling pains and I knew I would soon lose the child I carried. Daisy Curtis, the woman who acted as local midwife, layer-out-of-the-dead, and dispenser of country remedies, came to attend me. Her big, ungainly hands were surprisingly gentle while she worked.

"Please save my baby!" I begged. I owed this to Edward, no matter what he had done to me. "I must bear my husband a son."

She did not reply, and it was not until three hours later that I realized our fight had been in vain. The pains had left me and I slept. I was too tired to grieve; I think a curtain must have come down over my mind, sparing me the stark memory of recent events.

"He were a bad man," Daisy said as she tucked the blankets about me. "Spawn of the devil, that's what he was. But the gipsy got the better of him in the end. Like as not she'll rest quiet in her grave now."

"We didn't break the curse after all," I whispered, turning my head so that I could see the firelight reflected and gleaming in the pots which hung beside the fireplace. "Yasmin won . . . as she had intended."

Gabriel was constantly by my side. We both knew there was a secret between us, but the time was not yet ripe to speak of it. I knew instinctively who had been the cause of the fire, but I wanted him to tell me about it himself. I made no mention of his presence in Edward's bedchamber, but I knew why the village was speculating on the reason for the night man-hunt. The servants had spoken of my husband's anger against Gabriel, but no one knew the cause. Perhaps he had broken into the house, intent on theft, in order to revenge himself for his mother's death? The villagers dared not ask me direct, and I vowed that my own lips should remain firmly sealed.

It was in the early afternoon that Robert came to us. I was dozing when I became conscious of low voices in the kitchen. I recognized Daisy Curtis's tone and she seemed to be arguing hotly with someone. I opened my eyes and said:

"Who is it, Daisy?"

The light from the window was blocked

out by Robert's figure. I looked up at him and he knelt by my side, his large hands folding over mine.

"Thank God you're safe!" he whispered. "When I heard what had happened I could not rest until I had seen you for myself." His arms slid round my body and I leaned against his chest, weeping. "Dearest! I thought you had been killed with Edward. The pain . . . I cannot describe my fears . . . but you're here . . . you're safe?"

"Gabby found me and brought me from the house. He was wonderful."

"How did the fire start?"

"Perhaps I'll tell you . . . one day . . . when all this is over." My fingers sought his and tightened around them. "There will be no child."

"I know. Daisy told me. I am sorry."

I remained leaning against him, and I was comforted by his presence. I felt as if his strength flowed steadily from his body into mine, and I knew that I could not live without him.

"I wanted to bear the child," I murmured into Robert's jacket. "I wanted to break the curse. But Yasmin told me it wouldn't be my child. I didn't know what she meant, but I do now." I looked into his face. "Robert, she was there, you know. Edward thought it was me in the room, and ran to save me, but she tricked him." Robert stroked my hair and twined a lock around his left hand.

"You are still overwrought, my darling. You are imagining things."

"No Robert. I *saw* her! We all saw her . . . and she had made herself look like me!"

"Fire and shadow play strange tricks on the mind, dearest. There was no one in the room but Edward."

I did not argue; I was too tired. One day, I decided, I shall tell him all about Yasmin, but not now. He would never believe me.

Later that evening I asked to speak to Gabriel alone. Robert left the cottage with the woman who had offered me hospitality, and we had the place to ourselves.

"Gabby, sit beside me. I want to talk to you." I patted the edge of the bed. Gabriel lowered his eyes sheepishly. "Yes, Gabby, we must settle this matter for once and all; afterwards, we need never mention it again." He came to my side and sat down. I took his hands in mine and held them tightly.

"Gabby, I don't want to punish you in any way, but I *must* know what happened. Where did you go after you fled from my husband's bedchamber?"

"I . . . I knew many of the rooms were unused, and that not all of them were locked. I ran along the passage and into the far wing. Then I hid behind some furniture. I heard your husband, the Master, shouting for his servants and saw them from behind the shutters as they waited on the lawn to start their hunt for me. I knew he would kill me if he found me."

"Were you frightened, Gabby?"

"Yes, my lady. I thought that if I could hide in the house for a few days, you might help me escape."

"Weren't you afraid I might have told Sir Edward?"

"Oh no, my lady. I knew you wouldn't be doing that to me. You're too good. I thought I could stay in that room until your husband was far away; then I meant to come to you and ask for food."

"What made you change your mind?" I asked, filled with curiosity. I had not expected to learn that he had deliberately planned arson. There was something . . . or someone . . . behind this act. A swift lunge with a knife was in character; a planned attempt to burn down the house was not.

"I was in that room, my lady, when the other woman came to me."

I gasped. "Which other woman?" I think I knew before he told me who she would be.

"The one with the lovely dark hair. I thought I was alone in the room, but she was sitting at the table reading . . . or writing . . . I don't remember. She came to me and told me what I had to do."

"Did you not feel you should refuse?" I prompted gently.

"Oh no, my lady." He rubbed a hand over his eyes. "I felt strange; as if I were dreaming. I knew I must obey her orders. I saw the tinder box on the table and picked it up. 'Not this room', she said and I went out into the passage again. I found another room and set fire to the drapes. They burned very easily. I stood watching the blaze and laughed. It was so beautiful! I heard the woman laughing behind me and suddenly I came to my senses and realized what I had done! The fire was spreading with such speed that I was afraid for you, my lady. I heard the servants leave the house, shrieking and crying, but I thought of your safety, my dear lady." He bent low over my hands. "You know what happened next."

"Did you wonder about this woman?" I asked carefully. He nodded.

"Yes, my lady. I know who she was. I have seen a ghost."

"You *think* you saw one," I corrected. "There are no such things as ghosts." I wondered whom I was trying to convince, myself or him!

"If you say so, my lady, but I saw and talked to her like I now speak to you. She pretended to be you. That was why she was there."

"You did wrong not to allow me to call out to Sir Edward." I scolded, recalling the hand that had been clamped over my mouth. A sly expression came into Gabriel's eyes.

"Aie, my lady, perhaps I did, but it was what she would have wished. The ghost, I mean. It was right for him to be taken. An eye for an eye, like the Good Book says. Ma would have agreed. He took her life. I took his. Yet neither of us laid a hand on him. 'Twas meant that way, you see."

Somehow I understood. It was the way of Destiny.

"Ma was all I had in the world, my lady," he continued, tears filling his eyes. "She were good to me, and I loved her like I've loved no one else. I didn't have a Pa, you see, my lady. He died afore Ma could marry him. I do be a love-child, my lady," he finished proudly.

My hands trembled as I realized the full impact of his statement, and the words spoken by Mrs. Post came flooding back to me. Gabriel had been a love-child! Was this the child referred to by Yasmin? "A male child conceived in love . . . the seventh generation . . . ?" And all the time Edward had presumed this child to be one of his own body!

I lay back and shut my eyes while Gabriel studied me anxiously.

"You are tired, my lady."

"Yes, Gabby. Please leave me now. I promise you that this will remain a secret between us all our lives." I felt the kiss he implanted somewhat clumsily on the back of my hand.

We have often discussed this, Robert and I. Sometimes I take the gipsy charm from the box Robert bought me in Bodmin, and we look at it together, before returning it amongst the gifts so painstakingly made by the orphans I had left behind at Mrs. Crane's. I do not wear the charm now, because I know I do not need its protection.

As time has passed, I have been able to see the truth more clearly. Everything happened as Yasmin had planned. The Reynaulds had been cursed with a form of madness which did not die out until the seventh generation with Edward's own death. I was thankful not to have carried his child to full term . . . It, too, might have been tainted with that same madness.

In spite of Robert's protests that I was not yet strong enough, I insisted on attending Edward's funeral. I felt my place to be at his side, to the very last. I also requested that I be allowed to stand alone. He had been my husband for a few months, and our final parting should be affected with all the respect due a dead man.

The drizzle blew in thickly from the sea and the air was coldly harsh. I stood where I am standing today, but the hole was black and gaping. The villagers came in their droves to stare and whisper at the passing of the man they all hated. I had decided against burial in the family vault. Edward had set himself up as a man apart, a man with a mission . . . rather like Yasmin. I thought it fitting that he, too, should have a grave outside the vault; the only difference being that his should be marked by a granite stone.

I remained until the grave was covered, then I knelt to place my small bunch of late autumn blooms and leaves upon it.

"God grant you peace at last!" I whispered, and then rose to meet Robert who had been waiting some yards away.

★ ★ ★

It is strange to think how scared I was at returning here today! My visit to the house and the call to Yasmin when I asked her if all were well. It is so ridiculous! Time has healed old wounds.

The wealth that was left to me was not great because many of Edward's treasures had been destroyed in the fire. I have a manager at the mine and Robert visits there frequently to see how things are progressing. I made certain that all the cottages had their repairs carried out as swiftly as possible after the funeral, and I am glad to see how happy and contented are my people. Robert has spoken of rebuilding the Hall, but I could never live here again. The charred ruins would be a constant reminder. Perhaps we could find a site on the farther side of the village? It is time we left our present home six miles away. My two babies are proving more than a handful, and we need more room.

The past seems remote, part of another world in which I played an actress's role. It is strange, but sometimes I cannot believe I actually lived through those frightening months. The farther away the events, the more I realize that Yasmin existed only in my mind. I was undergoing a complete change in my mode of living, and such circumstances forced weird fancies upon me. I now believe that Edward honestly thought he had seen me at the window of my sitting-room. Gabriel, too, was undergoing a very emotional period of his life. He is very happy now, married to my Lily. He works in the mine and has a new cottage in the village. I had three new ones built. I think I shall return and call on my villagers. I can already hear their voices. I believe they are coming here to meet me! The children must have seen me standing in the lane looking at their homes . . .

Yes, they are coming. I must go and greet them.

But I cannot go until I have taken a final look at Edward's sad grave. It looks so forlorn and neglected. He was a man lacking in compassion, but I still feel a slight warmth for him. I will come back later and tidy the grave, ridding it of these clinging weeds. Perhaps I shall be able to pick some flowers from the hedgerows.

Others may have hated him, but not I . . . not now.

For how could I hate the man who gave me my dear Robert?

THE END

Other titles in the
Ulverscroft Large Print Series:

TO FIGHT THE WILD
Rod Ansell and Rachel Percy

Lost in uncharted Australian bush, Rod Ansell survived by hunting and trapping wild animals, improvising shelter and using all the bushman's skills he knew.

COROMANDEL
Pat Barr

India in the 1830s is a hot, uncomfortable place, where the East India Company still rules. Amelia and her new husband find themselves caught up in the animosities which seethe between the old order and the new.

THE SMALL PARTY
Lillian Beckwith

A frightening journey to safety begins for Ruth and her small party as their island is caught up in the dangers of armed insurrection.

THE WILDERNESS WALK
Sheila Bishop

Stifling unpleasant memories of a misbegotten romance in Cleave with Lord Francis Aubrey, Lavinia goes on holiday there with her sister. The two women are thrust into a romantic intrigue involving none other than Lord Francis.

THE RELUCTANT GUEST
Rosalind Brett

Ann Calvert went to spend a month on a South African farm with Theo Borland and his sister. They both proved to be different from her first idea of them, and there was Storr Peterson — the most disturbing man she had ever met.

ONE ENCHANTED SUMMER
Anne Tedlock Brooks

A tale of mystery and romance and a girl who found both during one enchanted summer.

CLOUD OVER MALVERTON
Nancy Buckingham

Dulcie soon realises that something is seriously wrong at Malverton, and when violence strikes she is horrified to find herself under suspicion of murder.

AFTER THOUGHTS
Max Bygraves

The Cockney entertainer tells stories of his East End childhood, of his RAF days, and his post-war showbusiness successes and friendships with fellow comedians.

MOONLIGHT
AND MARCH ROSES
D. Y. Cameron

Lynn's search to trace a missing girl takes her to Spain, where she meets Clive Hendon. While untangling the situation, she untangles her emotions and decides on her own future.

NURSE ALICE IN LOVE
Theresa Charles

Accepting the post of nurse to little Fernie Sherrod, Alice Everton could not guess at the romance, suspense and danger which lay ahead at the Sherrod's isolated estate.

POIROT INVESTIGATES
Agatha Christie

Two things bind these eleven stories together — the brilliance and uncanny skill of the diminutive Belgian detective, and the stupidity of his Watson-like partner, Captain Hastings.

LET LOOSE THE TIGERS
Josephine Cox

Queenie promised to find the long-lost son of the frail, elderly murderess, Hannah Jason. But her enquiries threatened to unlock the cage where crucial secrets had long been held captive.

THE TWILIGHT MAN
Frank Gruber

Jim Rand lives alone in the California desert awaiting death. Into his hermit existence comes a teenage girl who blows both his past and his brief future wide open.

DOG IN THE DARK
Gerald Hammond

Jim Cunningham breeds and trains gun dogs, and his antagonism towards the devotees of show spaniels earns him many enemies. So when one of them is found murdered, the police are on his doorstep within hours.

THE RED KNIGHT
Geoffrey Moxon

When he finds himself a pawn on the chessboard of international espionage with his family in constant danger, Guy Trent becomes embroiled in moves and countermoves which may mean life or death for Western scientists.

TIGER TIGER
Frank Ryan

A young man involved in drugs is found murdered. This is the first event which will draw Detective Inspector Sandy Woodings into a whirlpool of murder and deceit.

CAROLINE MINUSCULE
Andrew Taylor

Caroline Minuscule, a medieval script, is the first clue to the whereabouts of a cache of diamonds. The search becomes a deadly kind of fairy story in which several murders have an other-worldly quality.

LONG CHAIN OF DEATH
Sarah Wolf

During the Second World War four American teenagers from the same town join the Army together. Forty-two years later, the son of one of the soldiers realises that someone is systematically wiping out the families of the four men.

THE LISTERDALE MYSTERY
Agatha Christie

Twelve short stories ranging from the light-hearted to the macabre, diverse mysteries ingeniously and plausibly contrived and convincingly unravelled.

TO BE LOVED
Lynne Collins

Andrew married the woman he had always loved despite the knowledge that Sarah married him for reasons of her own. So much heartache could have been avoided if only he had known how vital it was to be loved.

ACCUSED NURSE
Jane Converse

Paula found herself accused of a crime which could cost her her job, her nurse's reputation, and even the man she loved, unless the truth came to light.

BUTTERFLY MONTANE
Dorothy Cork

Parma had come to New Guinea to marry Alec Rivers, but she found him completely disinterested and that overbearing Pierce Adams getting entirely the wrong idea about her.

HONOURABLE FRIENDS
Janet Daley

Priscilla Burford is happily married when she meets Junior Environment Minister Alistair Thurston. Inevitably, sexual obsession and political necessity collide.

WANDERING MINSTRELS
Mary Delorme

Stella Wade's career as a concert pianist might have been ruined by the rudeness of a famous conductor, so it seemed to her agent and benefactor. Even Sir Nicholas fails to see the possibilities when John Tallis falls deeply in love with Stella.

MORNING IS BREAKING
Lesley Denny

The growing frenzy of war catapults Diane Clements into a clandestine marriage and separation with a German refugee.

LAST BUS TO WOODSTOCK
Colin Dexter

A girl's body is discovered huddled in the courtyard of a Woodstock pub, and Detective Chief Inspector Morse and Sergeant Lewis are hunting a rapist and a murderer.

THE STUBBORN TIDE
Anne Durham

Everyone advised Carol not to grieve so excessively over her cousin's death. She might have followed their advice if the man she loved thought that way about her, but another girl came first in his affections.